KENDALL RYAN

The Play Mate

Copyright © 2017 Kendall Ryan

Copy Editing and Formatting by
Pam Berehulke

Cover Design by
Sara Eirew

Paperback Edition

About the Book

Smith Hamilton has it all—he's smart, good-looking, and loaded. But he remembers a time when he had nothing and no one, so he's not about to mess up, especially with his best friend's little sister. That means keeping Evie at arm's length . . . even though the once pesky little girl is now a buxom bombshell. A sexy blonde who pushes his self-control to the limit the night she crawls into bed with him.

Evie Reed knows she's blessed. She has an exclusive education, a family who loves her, and a new job managing social media for her family's lingerie company. But she wants more, like a reason to wear the sexy lingerie herself, and she has just the man in mind to help her with that. She's crushed on Smith forever. Surely, tricking her way into his bed will force him to see her in a new, adult way.

Except that when Evie's plan leads to disaster, she and Smith must decide. Should they ignore the attraction sizzling between them, or become play mates and risk it all?

Chapter One

Evie

My heart beat hot and fast and loud. Grabbing life by the balls would do that to a girl. I was standing right on the edge of something huge, and just needed the tiniest shove to jump in headfirst—if I was going to go through with this crazy plan.

"Come on, Evie," my best friend said, cheering me on. "Let him butter your croissant." Maggie giggled into her cloth napkin while I rolled my eyes.

"I'm not doing the nasty with some random stranger."

I had bigger goals in mind, loftier goals that involved indulging in carnal pleasures with the man I'd always desired. I wasn't some shy adolescent girl anymore. I was confident enough to admit what I wanted and go after it. This was going to be my gift to myself. A box to check off my bucket list before it was finally time to move on from my secret fantasies.

Maggie rolled her eyes. "I know. You've set your

sights on Smith."

It was the twenty-first century. A woman could take what she wanted sexually without feeling cheap or abused.

Smith Hamilton was my older brother's best friend. And come tomorrow night, he wouldn't know what hit him.

The feminist inside me beat on her chest and let out a battle cry.

I was doing this.

I would make Smith my bitch.

And zero fucks would be given.

I swirled the ruby-colored wine in my glass, a smile uncurling on my lips. "He's intelligent, well-educated, sinfully gorgeous, and unlike most guys our age, I'm betting he knows what he's doing in bed."

Maggie's glossy pink lips pulled into a smirk. "He is hot. I'll give you that."

It was our last night in the quaint French village where we'd hiked, sampled local wine, and gorged ourselves on crusty bread and soft cheese. Tomorrow we'd hop on a train to Paris. From there, Maggie would be flying home to start her new job, and I'd be enacting *Plan: Fuck Smith's Brains Out.*

Maggie and I had been backpacking our way through Europe for the past two weeks after graduating from college. To say we'd been sheltered at the all-girls school we'd attended would have been the understatement of the century. Now we wanted to sample all that life had to offer, and we were off to a pretty good start. I'd danced under the moonlight in Tuscany, dined on escargot in a French village, and risked my life climbing into the back of a motorbike taxi in Budapest. I'd seen world-famous landmarks and met local people. The one thing I hadn't done was achieve a non-self-assisted orgasm. Awkward, I know. But I had just the man in mind to change all that.

Nodding, I took another sip of my wine. Smith was hot. And tall. And sinfully sexy. I had to cross my legs to stifle the pressure building there.

I let out a sigh. *No.* This was just about sex. I wouldn't allow myself to pore over his every amazing quality, though there were many.

Even when I'd been an annoying little girl and he and my brother were teenagers, he'd been kind to me. While my brother had no problem yelling at me to get out of his room and slamming the door, Smith would drop to his knees so we were eye level and pat my head, saying if I left them alone for a little while, he'd come look at my pet frog later. He was always nice to me. Even when I probably didn't deserve it.

My doting parents and strict upbringing ensured that I was firmly on the straight-and-narrow path, and honestly, I did what was expected of me and never deviated. At the time, I'd thought it was the right thing to do, but now I was having major regrets. I didn't want to play by anyone else's rules anymore. I wanted to live my life my way. And that meant having the hot tryst I'd never been brave enough to pursue. I was almost giddy at the thought.

"Are you sure you want to do this with Smith?" Maggie asked, drawing me back to the present.

Ah, Smith. I let out a happy sigh. He was the thing all my teenage fantasies were made of. He was smart, sweet, and attractive. And he had this whole wounded alpha-male thing going on. He hid it well; most people would never know. But he was adopted as an older child, and I knew that his years spent in foster care longing for a forever family had shaped the man he was today. I was sure he wanted love and acceptance and belonging just as much as I did. Maybe even more.

"Of course." I'd never been more certain of anything in my entire life. "Why?"

Maggie chewed on her lip. "I'm just not sure if Smith is the man you should give it to. There's too many messy entanglements."

I shrugged. I'd been over all the pros and cons six thousand times already. Smith would be landing in Paris tomorrow to visit my brother, who was already there on business. I'd be joining them for dinner. There would be wine and conversation . . . and then later something sweeter than dessert. It was the perfect time. I couldn't have decided on a more magical first—okay, technically second—time if I tried. Paris was practically the world capital of romance. Nothing could go wrong.

And then we'd all go back to Chicago, which was a big enough city to avoid him if things turned weird afterward, like Maggie was convinced.

"No matter what, don't tell him you're practically still a virgin. It'll scare him off," Maggie added.

"First, I'm not a virgin. I did it with—"

She waved me off. "Yeah, I know. What's-his-name. That doesn't count."

"Why not? Of course it counts." I sat up straighter in my seat. *That so counted.*

Maggie rolled her eyes. "He didn't get you off. Didn't even try to put any romance into it. If there's no orgasm, it wasn't sex. You get a do-over. It's practically written in the Girl Code."

I thought over what she had said and decided that I liked that. A do-over. It went perfectly with my sassy new personality and my new take-no-shit philosophy.

"Wait, what do you mean? Don't guys like that? Being the first to conquer uncharted territory, and all that."

Maggie gave me a sorrow-filled look. "No, because smart men know that women get attached to their first.

Smith might be reluctant to go there with you." While my brain buzzed with thoughts of Smith, she continued. "There are so many expectations and emotions that go along with being someone's first. He might not be okay with that. And he might hurt you, and if I know Smith, he definitely wouldn't be okay with that."

That part was true. He'd always treated me with kid gloves.

"Fine. I won't tell him about what's-his-name, or that I need a do-over."

I'll just let him think I'm a sexual tigress on the prowl. That was much better than the depressing alternative, admitting that I'd never had an orgasm with a guy in all my twenty-two years.

But tomorrow night, that would all change.

And I couldn't wait.

Chapter Two

Smith

The first thing I saw when I walked into the bar was all those damn curves.

Full, round ones.

Tall, slim ones.

And my personal favorite—short, sturdy ones. Just right for three fingers of Scotch, neat.

I eyeballed the rocks glass like I could call it to me using my mind if I tried hard enough.

Hey, beautiful.

Come over here and see Daddy.

I slid my travel-weary body onto one of the empty stools and leaned on the glossy mahogany bar top with a groan. Jet lag from hell had my head throbbing like mad, and I waved the bartender over, hoping my rudimentary high school French would at least get me a drink.

"Uh, Scotch, *s'il vous plaît?*" I made a gesture to the bottle and waited hopefully.

The bartender shot me a broad grin in return and nodded his ponytailed head. "*Oui, monsieur.*"

I gave him a clipped nod of thanks and set my briefcase on the empty chair beside me.

It had been a hell of a day. My flight was delayed more than once, but I was bound and determined to get here. My buddy Cullen was counting on me, and there was no way in hell I was about to let him down. He'd been there for me since I was six years old. We'd skinned our first knees together. Shared our first beer together. Hell, our first kisses were even with the same girl. From as far back as then, no matter how much we both thought we liked her, even Suzie Hammerschmidt couldn't come between us.

Which meant I really needed to get my head out of my ass and stop thinking about Cullen's little sister, Evie.

I squeezed my eyes closed and scrubbed a hand over my face in frustration.

Fucking Evie.

She was seven years younger than us, but that never stopped her from wanting to be in our way, all the time. We used to call her Evie Knievel like the stunt guy, but it was done totally tongue in cheek. As kids, she'd follow us around wearing her shiny white shoes and little lace dresses, her honey-blond ringlets bouncing. The only time she ever unplugged her thumb from her mouth was to warn us that whatever it was we were about to do, we were going to get hurt doing it. Thinking on it now, I could feel a smile tugging at my lips.

"If you guys walk on that ice, you're gonna fall through and die."

"If you guys light those firecrackers, you're gonna blow your hands right off."

"If you guys try to climb that tree, you're gonna break your necks."

Only it had come out like *neckth* because she'd had a lisp when she was little. It was almost as annoying as she was, but looking back, it all seemed pretty adorable.

Not unlike Evie herself.

Shit.

The bartender slid the glass of amber liquid before me, and I nodded my thanks and took a deep pull. The liquor blazed a path of heat down the center of my chest and settled nicely into my stomach, radiating outward. For the first time since I'd left my house more than fifteen hours ago, the tension that had been knitting my neck and shoulder muscles together began to loosen.

It was either pop some pain reliever and go to bed, or hope the alcohol would put me in a pleasant haze. It wasn't even dinnertime, and I was meeting Cullen and his sister soon.

I needed to stop being such a chickenshit. This was no big deal. All I had to do was get through this dinner and brief visit, and Evie would be off backpacking with her friend again. Then Cullen and I could focus on the business at hand.

Simple.

I tugged out my cell phone to see if I'd gotten any messages since I arrived, but before I could scroll through, a loud voice echoed through the bar.

"Smith, you son of a bitch! It's so good to see you."

Cullen strode toward me, his infectious smile cranked up to an eleven. Despite that, there was no denying he looked harried. There were lines around his eyes I hadn't seen the year before, and dark smudges beneath them. As the king of workaholics, I recognized stress when I saw it, but we'd tackle that soon enough.

I stood and returned his man-hug before gesturing toward the empty seat next to me. "Good to see you too, man. It's been too long."

We'd done a good job of staying in touch over the years, but the last couple had been tough. Once Cullen took over the day-to-day running of his family's company, he worked hard to grow it enough that they could expand. And expand, they did. All the way to Paris. Now, though, they were going through some growing pains, and I was here to help him iron them out.

"I wish you'd let me pick you up at the airport," Cullen said, taking the offered chair and waving to the bartender. He held up one finger and then pointed at me before turning on the stool in my direction. "It would've been no problem to take off a little early."

"You say that, but you're obviously under a lot of

strain. I'm here to help, not add to that strain. Besides, it was a nice cab ride over. The driver spoke to me in French the entire time. I don't even think he realized I only understood about ten percent of what he'd said."

Cullen chuckled and then glanced at his watch. "Evie should be here any minute."

I took another swallow of Scotch and nodded without comment. It was stupid to half wish she'd be delayed and not make it at all. But call me stupid, because here I was, wishing it. Somehow over the past couple of years, annoying Evie had morphed into curvy, hot-as-hell, infiltrating-my-dreams Evie, and it was slowing killing me. On the flight over, when I should have been crunching numbers, I'd nodded off and promptly had the most erotic dream of my life.

We were at the lake near their family summer house, and even though I hadn't actually been there with Evie since she was around ten, dream Evie was all grown up. I was taking a swim on a moonlit night. She walked up to the water's edge wearing a man's dress shirt—*my* dress shirt—and nothing else.

My tongue stuck to the roof of my mouth as she

unbuttoned the shirt one painstaking button at a time. Almost in slo-mo, the sides of the shirt opened to reveal what had to be the most banging body of all time. Gorgeous, full tits. Hips big enough for my hands to get a good grip on, and trim, toned legs that were killing me because I couldn't decide whether I wanted them wrapped around my waist first or my face.

Evie.

I'd woken with a start right as she'd stepped into the water, buck naked, and pressed the full length of that soft body against my oh-so-hard one. And lucky thing I did, because things were about to get sticky in first class.

"You want to order a couple appetizers while we wait?"

I jerked my gaze back to Cullen and cleared my throat. "Sure, whatever you feel like."

Could I be more of an asshole right now? The guy was thrilled to see me after almost a year, and here I was, picturing his sister naked. Not that it had really been her body I was picturing. No possible way could she be that sexy under those clothes.

Could she?

Just as my blood started draining south again, I slammed the door on those thoughts and reached for my briefcase.

The best cure for sex on the brain was work.

"So, talk to me about what's going on at Sophia's. I ran through the numbers you sent me, and it seems like the expansion may have been a little premature." Sophia's was the lingerie company started by his grandmother when Cullen was still in diapers.

Cullen winced, but I held up a hand.

"Don't freak out. Things were looking really good, and it's not catastrophic. I think it can be fixed, but you're going to have to get creative. It would be a major plus if there was a way to increase sales before the end of the year in order to beef up cash flow a little."

"Funny you mention that," he said, taking a sip of his Scotch. "We're already looking at new sales avenues, expanding our reach on social media and trying some new advertising. That part's all still in its infancy. Before Nana died, she was against all of that. It was like pulling teeth for her to even consider monetizing the website. She was old school. She wanted people to come in and touch the fabrics, have the boutique experience. No matter a woman's body type or age, she wanted them to walk out feeling beautiful."

Cullen's smile was tinged with sadness, and for a second, I envied him. Yes, he'd lost his grandmother, but when she was alive, at least they'd had that close-knit bond. The whole Reed family did.

I had been lucky enough to get adopted at the age of six into a loving family, but my parents had been in their mid-fifties at the time, and my adopted siblings were all much older than me. I was really only close with my youngest sister, Pam. I loved them all dearly and would forever be grateful for all they'd done, but I'd always felt like I'd been missing something, always felt like the odd man out.

"This company was your grandmother's baby, and I want to make sure that we never lose that core concept. That's the brand. So we've got to maintain that personal feel of a boutique on the front end while making the back end function much more efficiently businesswise," I said, hoping I was calming his nerves.

I never imagined I'd be working with Cullen, but running a small part of my own family's well-oiled machine left me with some down time. I was the type who'd rather fill that time with something productive rather than laze around. I guess you could call me *type A*.

Cullen's grin widened and he shot me a wink. "That's where you come in. Can you help us figure out how to make the capital we do have stretch a little further to get us through the winter? Once spring arrives and all the fashion shows come to Paris, we're going to be golden. But for now?" He shrugged. "Things are lean."

I popped open my briefcase and pulled out the file folder I'd spent last week preparing. Then I slid it across the bar in front of him. He opened it and scanned the summary page quickly, and then shot me an incredulous glance.

"Seriously?" he asked. "Are you sure?"

"I'm as sure as I can be. Investing isn't an exact science, but I've got the capital to play with. I've looked at your holdings and the projections for spring, and I agree with you. Next year is going to be great. You just need a little help to get over the hump."

Cullen looked away for a second, the tension seeming to roll out of him in a wave as he blew out a breath. "I can't tell you what this means to me. It's ... it's everything, Smith. You're the best friend a guy could have. There's no one better."

The words felt like nails being hammered into my chest, one by one. *If I was such a good friend, I wouldn't be imagining your baby sister straddling my lap, or with something a lot bigger than her thumb in her mouth.*

But I kept my thoughts to myself because I was going to beat this thing. Not the over-aroused fucker in my pants. Although, depending on what Evie showed up wearing, I might have to beat that too.

No, I was going to beat this attraction to her. Wrestle it to the ground, put it in an arm hold, and make it my bitch.

And nothing was going to stop me. Not even sexy, curvy-hipped, Evie.

Chapter Three

Evie

I had the entire evening planned out to perfection, and my strategy was indestructible. I'd spent the past two hours showering, shaving, and blow-drying. My hair fell in soft waves down my back, and my makeup was subtle but skillfully applied.

I wanted to look flawless tonight. And not because I was vain, but because I'd worked so hard to get here. Losing the extra twenty pounds I'd always carried and growing my self-confidence in the process, I was finally ready for this moment.

This was my last hurrah before I finally let go of my crush on Smith and forced myself to grow up and move on with my life. I knew Maggie was right—of course this was a little crazy. But, damn it, this was what I wanted, and for once I was going to throw caution to the wind and just go for it.

Brushing one last coat of black mascara onto my lashes, I smiled at my reflection in the mirror.

One stupid, fumbling attempt at losing my virginity last year was the only experience under my belt. And I hadn't even gotten off.

I just wanted to have one orgasm that wasn't supplied by me. Was that too much to ask?

I'd been almost calculating in my planning of tonight, working out all the details in my mind. I knew Smith well enough to know that at dinner he'd drink two whiskeys, neat, and then switch to soda water with lime. I knew he'd thoroughly read the menu and ask about the specials, but he'd ultimately order the steak, medium, and a potato with sour cream but no butter.

After dinner when we all parted ways, my brother would step off the elevator to go to his room on the ninth floor while Smith and I rode up together to mine. Then I'd ask him if he would mind walking me to my room. It would seem an innocent enough request, and a normal thing to do for a woman traveling alone, right? Then when we're standing at the door, I'd invite him in. Being the polite gentleman he was, he'd accept, and then we'd have another cocktail and talk, and things would progress naturally from there.

I smiled at my reflection again. It was go time.

Only when I got downstairs to the hotel restaurant for dinner—nothing was like what I'd planned. Yes, my brother and Smith were here already, but rather than being seated at a table in the dining room, they were at the bar with glasses of wine in front of them.

Wine? Since when had Smith ever drank wine?

And even more concerning than the wine were the two busty blow-up Barbies practically in their laps.

Swallowing a sudden wave of nerves at the first sight of Smith I'd had in over a year, I took a deep breath.

His broad shoulders tugged at the material of his suit jacket, his long, powerful legs were stretched out before him, and his chiseled jaw was in need of a good shave. His hair was a bit longer then I remembered on top. *Something to grab onto.* I smiled.

When I got closer, I could see the woman standing beside Smith had her hand curled around his bicep. She was sipping a drink, flirting . . . encroaching on my territory.

What the hell? This wasn't a scenario I'd planned for.

Pulling a deep breath in my lungs, I stopped between my brother and Smith.

"Gentlemen," I purred, my gaze finding Smith's and then dropping away in a way I hoped was sexy. Then again, I'd spent far too much time reading the sex tips in *Cosmo* magazine but no time actually practicing them, so it was entirely possible I looked like a cross-eyed, sex-starved weirdo.

"Evie," Smith's deep voice boomed, his smile blossoming into something full and genuine.

His hazel eyes locked on mine, and I felt a shiver race down my spine.

"Hi, Smith," I said, my voice shaky.

"Hey, sis. You finally made it." Cullen rose to his feet and gave me a brotherly one-armed hug. "This is Francesca and Giada. They're here for the fashion show."

Of course they were models. It was the universe's cruel joke at my expense. Standing next to the two of them, I suddenly felt that twenty pounds I'd worked so hard to lose should have been forty.

"Join us. Would you like a cocktail?" Smith asked. "Or a glass of wine?" When I squinted at him, he shrugged. "When in Rome." Then he raised his glass to his perfectly plump, full lips and took a long swallow, the thick column of his throat working.

Signaling the bartender, I ordered the strongest thing I could think of. "A martini, please."

He nodded and scurried off to grab the bottles that would give me the liquid courage I needed.

Smith chuckled low under his breath beside me. "Are you sure you don't want a Sex on the Beach?"

I looked at the pink cocktail in front of his *date* and shook my head. "I'm good. Thanks."

Apparently Francesca and Giada didn't speak much English, but that didn't stop them from communicating in sultry glances and suggestive body language with the guys.

Smith laughed at something Francesca said and patted her hand like he had no idea what she was talking about, but he was amused nonetheless.

If I had one ounce of the self-confidence and charm these women had, I wouldn't be in this position in the first place. A knot formed in the pit formed in my stomach.

Why the hell was Smith so enamored with her anyway? She had entirely too much makeup on, and he acted like her ordering a Sex on the Beach was the most interesting thing in the world. I could order a froufrou drink too, but that didn't make me special or interesting.

As I stared straight ahead at the bottles lining the shelves behind the bar, anger bubbled up inside me. A wave of fresh laughter broke out when the women were trying to inquire, I thought, if Donald Trump was actually the president.

After sucking down half my martini, I set it down with a shaking hand. "You know what?" I said, turning toward my brother and Smith. "I thought we were going to have dinner, but if you guys want to play grab-ass instead, I'm out of here."

Plucking my clutch from the bar, I rose to my feet. *Forget this.* I knew what I wanted, but I wasn't going to be anyone's pushover.

Smith stood too. "Hey, don't go."

His hand came to rest on my lower back, and since my dress was backless, his warm fingers landed on my bare skin. My eyes sank closed, and I felt my knees tremble.

When I opened my eyes, Smith's hazel ones were locked on mine, looking apologetic.

"Evie's right. Come on. Let's go to dinner. We don't want to lose our reservation," he added, pulling his gaze from mine and casting a glance at my brother.

My mouth lifted in a smile. I was relieved and a little surprised that he actually noticed I was mad, given that Francesca had been pressing her large fake boobs against his arm while she grinned at him.

As Smith tossed a couple of bills onto the bar, Cullen reluctantly rose to his feet. "Yes, I guess it's that time."

Just as the hostess approached to lead us to our table, I saw Francesca scribble down her number on a cocktail napkin and shove it in Smith's pocket.

Taking a deep, calming breath, I followed the hostess

to our table, my hips swishing seductively. I could have sworn I felt Smith's gaze on my ass. Maybe that number in his pocket meant nothing. Maybe I could still try to salvage tonight.

At our table, we were looking at our menus when Cullen cleared his throat. "I would like to make a special announcement concerning the company."

Smith raised his glass. "No business talk tonight, brother. We're in Paris for what could be a once-in-a-lifetime trip. Let's just enjoy this good food, good wine, and good company."

I smiled at him and took the last swallow of my martini. I assumed that Cullen's big announcement was that Smith was going to become a financial backer in the company. It was something Cullen had mentioned before, taking on an investor. And since I knew Smith was a numbers guy, it was no small mystery that he'd be a silent partner—funding our next round of purchase orders, if it came to that.

Cullen nodded approvingly. "Fine. There will be plenty of time for work talk later."

"Then cheers," Smith said, his glass still raised. "To old friends."

We clinked glasses, which were now mostly empty.

"Shall we order another bottle?" Smith drained the last drop of his wine and met my gaze.

"I'm game if you are."

Though unspoken, I couldn't help the deep wave of satisfaction I felt at the desire building between us.

Cullen signaled the waitress and ordered a bottle of merlot while Smith continued studying me from across the table. The wine was delivered with three fresh glasses and a loaf of warm bread, and since my stomach was tied up with nerves, I would have been fine with just this for dinner. Merlot and a good crusty bread? That was my idea of heaven. No way I could survive on one of those no-carb diets.

When the waitress returned, Smith asked about the specials and listened attentively, then ordered the steak. I smiled. My night was back on track.

Throughout the meal, I couldn't help but notice the

weight of Smith's stare on me, the flash of heat I felt when his gaze roamed along my skin. Even little things about him—like the way his lips closed around his fork— enthralled me, and it was maddening.

Finally, dinner was done, the last of the plates cleared away, and I was ready to pull a page from my playbook and enact *Plan: Fuck Smith's Brain Out.*

As my brother and Smith fought over the check, I excused myself to the restroom, needing to quickly relieve myself and check my appearance. After all, there'd be nothing worse than trying to get your freak on only to realize you had a piece of spinach between your teeth. Considering I hadn't even eaten spinach, it would be especially troubling.

Rinsing my hands at the sink, I gazed up at my reflection in the mirror.

Am I sure about this?

I remembered that Maggie had told me most men preferred a woman shaved bare. But that was just too bad. I wasn't going to change who I was for a man. I was neatly trimmed, and that would have to be good enough.

I ran through all the details in my mind. I had already tucked a condom inside the zippered pocket in my purse. Applying one last swipe of nude lip gloss, I gave myself a satisfied nod.

Not about to let my self-confidence waver now, I held my head high and strutted from the restroom. Back inside the restaurant, I spotted Cullen alone at our table as I approached.

"Where's Smith?" I asked, stopping beside my brother.

Cullen stifled a yawn. "He said he was tired. I think the time difference is messing with him."

He up and left? Just went to bed? He clearly didn't read the fuck-me signals I was shooting him with my eyes all night.

Men.

I rolled my shoulders, needing to relieve the pressure I felt building.

Panicking internally, I plastered on a neutral expression and let my brother escort me to the elevator and up to my room, all the while my mind worked overtime. *What am I going to do now?*

Once in my room, I punched out a text to Maggie, pacing the floor as I waited for her reply.

Several minutes passed until I realized that it was four in the morning back home and a response wasn't coming. Not anytime soon, at least.

This was it, now or never. And I wasn't about to squander this opportunity.

I knew what I needed to do.

It was time to be bold.

Drawing a deep breath into my lungs, I headed toward the elevator again. But this time, my destination was the hotel lobby, where I prayed I could convince the hotel staff that I was the wife of Smith Hamilton and had lost my room key.

Chapter Four

Smith

All in all, it had been a damned good night.

I closed the lid on my travel grooming case, my teeth minty fresh and flossed, before heading back into the bedroom of my hotel suite.

I'd gotten to hang out with Cullen, which was always fun. We'd managed to talk some business, and we were both on the same page there. Plus, I'd met a couple of women, one of whom might make my stay a little less lonely at night. So, why the fuck was I restless?

I climbed into bed feeling edgy and out of sorts, and considered grabbing my laptop. Maybe work would settle me down some. Lord knew we had enough ahead of us if I really wanted my bail-out plan to work well enough to help Cullen's company. He'd busted his ass building it to what it had become, and to have him fail now would be devastating. He'd always had my back, and I was going to do my damnedest to return the favor.

I'd just reached for my computer bag when I caught

sight of the napkin on the nightstand and smiled.

Francesca's number. But that wasn't what had me grinning. It was recalling the pissy way Evie had reacted when she thought she was being ignored that made me want to laugh out loud. She'd always been like that, quick to tell us exactly how she felt about any and every situation.

Little Evie.

Not so little anymore, my cock reminded me with a twitch.

I shifted under the sheets and gave my balls a warning squeeze. None of us should be thinking about her right now. Yeah, so maybe she'd finally graduated from college, but she would always be Cullen's baby sister, and a birthday cake or a diploma wasn't going to change that.

Then why did she have to torture me by looking so hot?

I could almost hear Evie's snappish reply to that. *Yeah, it's all about you, Smith.*

I grinned again despite myself, and flicked off the light. There was no point in beating myself up about it. I'd never act on it, and it wasn't like we had to spend a lot of time together. A little time and space, and I'd forget all about her. Chicago was a big city, and once we were back home, I doubted I'd be seeing much of her.

The second I closed my eyes, though, the way she'd looked came flooding back, bringing a hot rush of blood to my cock along with it. It wasn't just the clothes, although they didn't hurt. Her low-cut dress had clung to every wicked curve, leaving me wondering if she'd even been wearing a bra. I'd have given my left nut to check and see . . . until she turned around and I noticed the damned thing was backless.

I let out a growl and flipped my pillow over to the cold side. Evie had always been a good girl. In fact, I distinctly remembered her telling me that she was still a virgin just over a year before. Who made it through more than half of their college life without fucking someone?

Evie, that was who.

She hadn't meant to tell me. It had come out in a drunken ramble on the night of her twenty-first birthday.

Cullen and I had taken her out, and she got plastered after sucking down her weight in sugary Sex on the Beach cocktails. I probably should have stopped her, but it was a rite of passage, and I wasn't about to be a killjoy. Besides, it was kind of fun to see her taking risks and being a little wild for once.

She'd spilled her guts in more ways than one that night. The only saving grace was that she didn't seem to remember most of it. I'd thrown a little test her way when I'd mentioned the drink to her at dinner tonight, and she didn't even flinch. Probably for the best. She'd wound up hunched over the toilet at the local bar with me holding her hair. If she knew how the night had ended, I was sure she'd be mortified.

I shoved away the oddly fond memory and yanked the sheet down to my waist, feeling suddenly overheated. No more thinking about Evie. I was in town to do a job, and I wasn't going to stop until it was done. Anything else was a distraction I didn't need.

I closed my eyes, but my muscles were still tense. Eventually, though, the drinks and the jet lag caught up with me. My mind drifted, and soon enough, my eyes slid shut. The stress of the day faded away, and I could almost feel myself slipping into dreamland.

The sound of water tickled my ears, luring me from darkness toward the lake I'd dreamed of on the plane. I stood at the water's edge, bathed in moonlight, when a naked Evie emerged.

Her breasts were high and full, her waist nipped in and trim enough to span with my hands . . . hands that itched to touch her. She moved toward me, closing the distance between us. Her smile was sweet but a little wicked as she reached out and wrapped those lean, elegant fingers around my throbbing cock.

I bucked forward and groaned, arching my hips into her tentative grasp. *Fuck, yeah.* No guilt here. Only a wizard could control their dreams, and I was nobody's wizard.

Her grip tightened as I laid my hand over hers, urging her to work my shaft up and down in long, slow strokes.

"Jesus," I growled, reaching up to fist my hand in her hair.

It was that . . . the sound of my own voice, that

brought me fully back to consciousness. The pond and naked Evie in the moonlight were gone, but the hand on my cock? Still at it, and doing a fine fucking job.

Francesca.

A slow smile tugged up my lips. She must have figured out a way to bribe the front-desk clerk to let her into my room. It was a ballsy move, but I didn't hate it. Especially now, as she straddled my thighs.

I'd heard that French women were more sexually forward.

Viva la France!

Totally not how I'd expected to end the night, but I'd gone to bed all keyed up and could use the release. No chance I'd be kicking a gorgeous woman out of my bed, whether she'd broken some laws to get in it or not.

I reached up and spanned her waist in my hands, letting out a groan as I realized her skin was bare. It was too dark to see, but my fingertips were doing a fine job of cataloging what my eyes couldn't.

"You're killing me," I muttered. Now that I'd

released her hand, her strokes grew tentative, more languid, and the need for more was clawing at me hard. "Tease."

Her breathy laugh was more like a gasp as I let my fingers trail up her sides to brush against the underside of her breasts. Strange, I had remembered them being larger. Almost too large for her body, but as I cupped her tits now, they felt just right. The full, soft globes fit perfectly in my hands, her nipples taut in my palms as I caressed her.

She moaned softly under her breath, the sound almost like a relieved sigh. The motion of her hand increased as I plucked one nipple between my thumb and forefinger. Her hips started rocking against my thighs, and her breathing grew choppy.

"So responsive, just how I like it," I managed through gritted teeth. "That feel good, baby?"

She moaned a noise of affirmation, and that was good enough for me.

"Now, stroke that dick, sweetheart," I said on a groan.

Her careful strokes were torture. She wasn't going to hurt me. In fact, I didn't mind when sex got a little rough.

I released her breasts and removed her hand from my shaft. After placing a wet, open-mouthed kiss against her palm, I wrapped it back around me, groaning when her grip tightened possessively and pumped again.

I sat up, and her scent surrounded me. It had been more cloying at the restaurant. Now, though, she smelled sweet. Like hotel soap and something citrusy. I buried my face into her neck and breathed deeply before closing my teeth over the spot where her pulse fluttered wildly.

"Mmm . . ."

She released my cock and pressed in closer, curling her arms around my neck and resting her forearms on my shoulders.

I nibbled and sucked, reveling in the feel of her soft chest crushed against my hard one.

The rocking grew more insistent and had become more of a slow grind. The rhythm was inconsistent and a little hesitant, so I took control, cupping her round hips in my hands and using them to work her over my straining erection. Her silky panties were soaked, heating me to the point of combustion as I tore my mouth from her neck and slanted it over her lips.

Jesus, those lips. So plump and sweet and soft. Kissing her was like heaven. I could only imagine what that mouth would feel like wrapped around my swollen cock. I dug my fingers into her hips and increased the pace, needing the pressure . . . knowing she needed it just as badly.

She threw her head back and let out a muffled moan that sounded like a plea.

If she wanted more, then I wouldn't deny her.

I slid her off me and hooked a finger inside those wet little panties, snapping the slender string that held them together with one tug.

She gasped as I pressed her back against the mattress, and I only wished I could see her body as I slid down the bed and hunkered down between her thighs. I traced her silky skin from hip to hip, letting my fingers drop lower with each pass. By the time I nudged her slick clit with my thumb, she was close to sobbing.

"Shh, it's okay, " I murmured, making sure my warm breath feathered her pussy as I spoke. "I'm going to take good care of you."

I could hear her head tossing restlessly against the pillow as I passed my thumb over her again, groaning when I encountered that wet heat.

"Jesus, you're soaked for me," I said, my cock bucking against the mattress with the need to get inside her.

Her breath was coming so fast now, it sounded like she'd run a marathon. I dipped my face lower until a tiny swatch of downy hair tickled my lips. Then I took a long, deep lick.

"Ahhhh!"

Vaguely, I realized her voice sounded different, but I imagined mine did too. Lust did that to a person. Before I could think on it for another second, her hips shifted hesitantly, pressing her pussy directly into my mouth.

Perfect.

I gripped her hips and dived in, licking and sucking

with abandon. Soft and gentle for a second, and then drawing long and hard on that sweet little clit.

Her legs were so tense, all her muscles tight, and I knew she was close. I pulled back an inch and encouraged her in a low voice. "That's it, babe. Come for me."

A second later, my tongue was back in action. Her hips moved frantically in time with my now-rhythmic sucking. Her thighs clamped over my face, and she let out a long, low scream.

"Yesss!"

Blood pounded in my ears as she disintegrated all around me. Her scent filled my nostrils and her cries swamped my senses as she quaked and shook. Somewhere in the back of my mind, I realized she'd said *yes* and not *oui*, but I was too far gone to give a shit. My balls were drawn up tight, hot liquid snaking up the length of my shaft, ready to fire.

As the aftershocks of her delicious orgasm faded, I dragged my mouth away from her and lunged for the bedside table. I plucked out a condom and wrestled it onto my pulsing cock in record time.

She was still trembling when I slid between her thighs again and pressed the head of my dick against her wet heat. "You sure you want this?"

Her head bobbed up and down where it was tucked in against my throat.

I took it slow, knowing she was likely sensitive from the first climax, feeding her just the tip and then a little more.

"Jesus, that's tight. Fuck." I growled, pressing my forehead to hers.

I could have come just like that from the grip of her wet cunt, but I wasn't going out like that. She'd done all the work by coming up here—the least I could do was offer up a double play. I was still trying to talk myself down a little when she let out a strangled cry and thrust her hips upward, wedging me in until my cock was buried to the hilt, and she released a tense cry.

A dozen thoughts hit me at once, but only a few of them mattered. Francesca's pussy was like a boa constrictor strangling my cock.

It was sublime.

It was amazing.

And it was definitely not Francesca.

My pulse jackhammered wildly as the truth hit me, but it wasn't until I used every last ounce of strength I had to pull away, which was no easy feat, and flip on the light that I knew for sure.

Evie.

She blinked up at me, her face flushed, her eyes full of guilt, her honey-colored hair mussed.

From you fucking her, you piece of shit.

Christ, Cullen was going to murder me. My stomach dropped to my feet.

"What the actual fuck, Everleigh?" I demanded, leaping to my feet.

My cock bobbed out in front of me, still as hard as granite despite the shock of a lifetime. I was staring down the barrel of the world's worst case of blue balls, but I scaled back my shock and anger when I saw the tears in her eyes.

I grabbed the top sheet and covered her with it, but not before I got an eyeful of the most glorious set of tits and the sweetest, pinkest little cunt I'd ever seen. Talk about wet dreams . . . I'd never be able to get that sight out of my head now.

I closed my eyes and sucked in a steadying breath before blowing it out. When I opened my eyes, Evie was crawling backward to lean against the headboard, looking miserable.

"I'm sorry," she whispered, shaking her head as she toyed with the edge of the sheet. "I don't know what came over me."

It was you who came over me, I almost snapped back. But damn if I would change that. She'd been so hot, so ready . . .

This was Evie. Cullen's little sister.

I bent over and searched the floor until I found a discarded bathrobe she must have worn for the walk from her room to mine.

"Here," I said, irritated to find my voice still husky with need.

I yanked off the barely used condom and pulled on a pair of boxers while I waited with my back turned until she'd shrugged on the robe I'd given her.

"Okay, you can turn around," she said softly.

I did, and sat on the edge of the bed, my mind still reeling. "What were you thinking, Evie?" I was dying to know.

Her throat worked as she swallowed hard. "I'm grown now, Smith. I'm an adult, and I don't know what it feels like to be with a real lover. That's ridiculous. I made a plan, and this is what I wanted."

"So, why me?"

She shrugged and looked away. "Because I like you. I trust you. And I admire you. So, why not you?"

There were worse reasons, I couldn't deny that, and her words took the edge off my anger. I almost wanted to pull her in and give her a hug, but my dick had finally stopped throbbing and I wasn't about to poke the bear.

"I just want to be part of the real world and start experiencing life. I was always on you guys for trying new things and being so daring. I sort of wished I could be like that for once."

I wished it too. Especially now that I'd had a taste of her.

"Your brother would hate me. And he might even kill me," I said, holding her wide-eyed gaze. "But I think you're gorgeous, and whoever you wind up doing this with is a lucky son of a bitch."

Oddly, in that moment, I hated the motherfucker, and he was only hypothetical. I shoved aside the ridiculous feeling and pressed on.

"Anyway, as much as I would love to show you the ropes, it can't happen between us. But this doesn't change anything. You and I are still friends for life, all right?"

"Yeah, okay." She nodded and eyed me for a long moment. "So, probably bad timing, but . . . what am I going to do now?"

I scrubbed a hand over my face and shrugged helplessly. "You know what, Evie? Maybe talk to a friend or a pastor, someone like that. I don't think we should be having this conversation, regardless of what just happened. Let's get things back on the right track. The friend track."

"Sure, no, I know," she said, pushing herself to her feet and nodding furiously. "I should go anyway. I've got a lot to do tomorrow. And look, I'm really sorry. I hope you can forgive me."

"Forgiven," I said as I walked her to the door.

But not forgotten.

She stepped into the hallway and gave me a tiny wave before scurrying down the hall and disappearing into the elevator.

Now all I had to do was fall asleep and not dream about Little Evie Reed, who had just rocked my fucking world. Because if I couldn't get her out of my head and her brother found out?

I'd be a dead man.

Chapter Five

Evie

So. Embarrassed.

I was embarrassed at Smith's stinging rejection, but ten thousand times worse than that? My own idiotic behavior. I couldn't believe how stupid I'd been. I'd failed spectacularly last night, and the sting of white-hot shame was burning a hole in my chest.

I winced as I rolled out of bed. *Jeez.* I hadn't even technically had sex, but my vagina didn't know it. I was sore and tender deep inside. And not to mention filled with regrets.

Seriously, who botches their first (okay, second) time so badly they can't convince the guy to follow through?

Barefoot, I padded toward the bathroom and shed my pajamas while I waited for the water to heat. Utterly ashamed of myself, I shampooed, conditioned, and scrubbed until I was pink all over.

I'd sobbed quietly last night when I got back to my

room until I'd cried myself to sleep. But today was a new day, and thankfully, I didn't have to face Smith. It was the only silver lining in this shit show.

Last night, I'd entered his room and lain with him in the bed. His breathing was deep and even, and I knew he was asleep. I didn't see any harm in cuddling close to him. I wasn't sure if anything else would happen, but then it did. He responded to my touch, and then I grew bolder, and before I knew what was happening, I was reaching under the sheet and stroking the longest, thickest cock I'd ever felt. Things happened quickly after that. He'd removed my robe, sucked on my nipples until I was soaking wet with need. His fingers in my panties moved with such certainty. He was all man, and it showed. Experienced where I was unsure.

I came quickly and wanted more. I was nearly dizzy from his kisses, his touches, and then he was sheathing himself in a condom and asking me if I was sure. I'd never been more certain of anything in my entire life. And then he entered me, pushing past my tight walls, and the stretch had stung but felt wonderful, all at the same time.

Until he'd stopped suddenly and pulled away.

Wrapped in a robe with my hair fashioned in a turban, I sat down on the bed and grabbed my phone. I thought about texting Maggie, but what could I say? That she'd been right all along? *Jesus.*

I didn't have to tell Smith that I was nearly still in virgin territory—he knew. He just somehow knew. Did it feel as amazing for him as it did for me? Probably not, or he wouldn't have pushed me away like he'd been burned.

As I stared down at my phone, contemplating what to do, a text from my brother popped up.

CULLEN: Come down for breakfast. We're at the restaurant across from the lobby.

He and Smith were down there. No way I was joining them. If needed, I'd fake an illness—traveler's diarrhea. That was a thing, right?

Except then my brother would come up here and check on me, pull the concerned-older-brother card, and Smith would know the truth—that I was too ashamed to face him.

Well, fuck that. I wouldn't give him the satisfaction. I would go down there and be confident and calm about the whole thing—the epitome of maturity, when I felt anything but—and then we'd all go home soon and I'd never have to see Smith again.

I responded to Cullen's text, telling them to wait for me before they ordered. Then I blow-dried my hair and perfected my makeup until I was satisfied that I looked good enough that Smith would regret calling off our little fuck fest last night.

I hated that I knew exactly what those full lips felt like sucking and licking my tender flesh, hated that I knew he could make me come in about two minutes flat, hated that I only got to feel him for the briefest of moments.

But most of all, I hated myself for being so stupid. I couldn't believe I thought my plan would actually work, that I'd waltz in there and seduce him. Christ, he could have probably pressed assault charges if he really wanted to.

I had no idea what to say or how to act when I saw

Smith, but I was going to put on a brave face and give it my best shot.

The extra concealer I applied took care of those big dark circles under my eyes from tossing and turning rather than sleeping last night. Then I dressed in a pair of dark skinny jeans that fit me like a glove, and a low-cut red sweater that showed off what little cleavage I had. Black stiletto boots and a swipe of nude lip gloss, and I was ready.

Eat your heart out, Smith Hamilton. *You jackass.*

Chapter Six

Smith

Damn.

I'd been trying my hardest to chat breezily with Cullen like it was any other day. But the second Evie stepped into the restaurant, it was like the air was sucked out of me.

Sure, I'd spent half the night aching and wanting until I'd finally succumbed and jerked off to the image of her legs spread on my bed, her pussy glistening.

And, sure, I'd spent my morning trying to forget it ever happened.

But none of those things seemed to help when her gaze skimmed past her brother and landed on me. Her cheeks turned a pretty shade of rose, telling me her thoughts were as dirty as mine. My cock stood at half-mast, and I cleared my suddenly dry throat.

Jesus, it's going to be long day.

I'd had half a mind to march down to her room last

night and demand to know what in the fuck she'd been thinking, but since I didn't fully trust myself not to suggest that we pick up where we left off, I'd stayed put.

Cullen stood and waved his sister to an empty chair on the opposite side of the table. "Hey, sis."

"Hey, guys," she mumbled back.

She looked gorgeous, all freshly showered and made up. I was fairly certain she'd made the extra effort just to torture me.

"Good morning, sunshine. You look nice today," I found myself murmuring with a slow grin. "Had a good night's sleep, did you?"

The dark, poorly concealed smudges underneath her eyes answered that question, but I couldn't help myself. I hadn't intended to tug her pigtails today. In fact, I'd planned to do my level best to ignore her and keep things super polite but distant. And then I saw her face, and the devil climbed up onto my shoulder and took over. If I had to suffer because of her antics now that I couldn't get her naked body out of my mind, there was no reason I should have to do it alone.

Her eyebrows drew into a frown and she opened her mouth, only to glance at Cullen and snap it shut a moment later. She took a deep breath and gave me a sweet smile in return, but there was no mistaking the warning in her eyes.

"I'm doing great, and yes, it was a totally uneventful night. A real snoozer, so I slept like a baby. Thanks for asking."

I had to hold back a bark of laughter. She'd always had a sharp little tongue, only now I'd heard it *and* tasted it. And oddly enough, I wanted more of both.

You're playing with fire, Smith.

Didn't I know it? I'd played with it last night, and I couldn't deny it had been one of the sexiest experiences of my life. Despite my rational mind telling me nothing good could come of it, I couldn't stop myself from seeing just how far I could press.

"I would've slept better, but the room was a little . . . *tight*. Was your room tight, Evie?"

She let out a strangled cough, and Cullen looked up from the file he'd been reading and gestured to the water pitcher between them.

"Yes, Evie, have a drink, won't you? We haven't ordered yet, aside from beverages. There's water and coffee here . . . or would you prefer a *virgin* mimosa?" I raised my brows innocently as I asked the question, but her face ramped up from rosy pink to tomato red.

"Um, is—isn't that just plain orange juice?" she stammered, tucking a lock of honey-colored hair behind one ear.

I pretended to consider the question and then nodded. "Yeah, I guess it is. Would you like some?"

She shook her head and muttered something under her breath that sounded suspiciously like *asshole*, but before I could process it, Cullen closed the folder he'd been thumbing through and laid both of his hands on the table.

"First, I want to say that I'm so glad you're both here. It's super important to me that you guys care enough to come and rally around me and the business in our hour of need." He turned to his sister and gave her a fond grin. "Evie, Nana would be so proud of you and the woman you've become. And Smith, seriously, I couldn't ask for a better friend. All this to say, I'm thrilled because—"

The cell phone next to Cullen's file folder chirped, and he held up a finger as he glanced down at it. "Hold that thought. This is our distributor in London, and I need to take it. Give me ten."

He shot up from his chair and crossed the dining room before ducking out into the hallway as he pressed the phone to his ear. "Yeah, it's me. What's going on?" He continued out of sight, leaving Evie and me sitting there staring at each other.

No point in pretending like it hadn't happened. Best to get it out in the open so we could move on.

We both started speaking at once.

"Look, I—"

"What do you think y—"

When she paused, I waved her on with a flourish of my hand. "Please, go ahead. As you know, my motto is *always* ladies first."

In her case, it had been ladies only, but who was counting?

My cock flexed behind my zipper in a not-so-subtle reminder that someone was, indeed, counting.

Her jaw clenched, and she pounded the table with one fist. "Cut the crap. You know exactly what you're doing."

I blinked back at her and shrugged. "I'm not sure what you mean."

"The *virgin* mimosa? And the *tight* hotel rooms? What the hell is wrong with you? It's like you want Cullen to find out. Do you know how pissed he'd be?" she demanded, her chest heaving hard enough for her breasts to push against her sweater in the most mouthwatering way.

For a second, I blacked out as memories of the night before flitted through my mind like an X-rated movie. Evie, grinding on top of me. Biting her lip as she cried out in pleasure. The tight grip of her channel squeezing me, pulling at my cock, practically begging me to explode and fill her with hot cum.

"Smith?" She snapped her fingers in front of my face. "Hellooo?"

I tugged at my shirt collar, wishing I'd skipped the tie today. "Yep, I'm here. Sorry, I was just having a very vivid flashback."

She scowled at me, her hand shaking as she turned over her coffee mug for the waitress who had paused at our table with a steaming carafe.

"Cullen is not going to find out. He's not going to know that you have the world's tightest teacup."

"What the hell is wrong with you? Can we not discuss this?" she hissed.

"Excuse me, sugar tits, I'm sorry. I'm a bit fucking thrown off here. How did you want me to act this morning . . . like you weren't naked and wet and grinding on my dick last night?"

She grinned, but it was fake and didn't reach her pretty eyes. "Yeah, that'd be super helpful."

I could have barked out a laugh, but I knew based on her reaction, Evie didn't find this situation nearly as funny as I did.

She lifted the coffee mug to her lips with a trembling hand and then paused, still looking straight at me. "Just do me a favor and forget last night ever happened."

Yeah, right. Not possible.

I couldn't seem to stop my brain from remembering all the wonderful soft, pleasant things about her. The way she felt underneath me, her scent, how quickly she climaxed, almost like she'd been desperate for it . . .

My cock pulsed again.

Christ.

"How's this . . . I'll forgive you for breaking into my room. But forgetting last night? There's not a chance in hell of that happening."

"Argh!" She buried her flaming face in her hands. "Can you please? Pretty please? I just want to forget that ever happened, and I want you to as well. Wipe it from your brain. Is that too much to ask?"

I let my gaze travel over those curves, so delicious they should be illegal, and again, my mouth started moving before my brain weighed in.

"Actually, I can't. I won't ever forget the feeling of you coming on my face. The way your thighs gripped my cheeks as you shuddered for me. And frankly?" I let my gaze trail down the front of her sweater where her nipples had hardened, peaking against the soft fabric. "I don't think you can forget it either. But you're welcome to try."

Her lean throat worked as she swallowed, and suddenly the room—and my pants—seemed much too small.

"Now you're all clear to bang that chick from the bar. Consider that my gift to you." Evie spread her napkin on her lap, a sour expression on her face.

"How generous of you." It was a prize of little consolation. I had no interest in that. Whatsoever. Which was fucking weird.

"Good news," Cullen said, sailing back into the restaurant and toward our small table. "Everything's on track in London. Now we can get back to business." His gaze flicked between Evie and me, and he frowned. "You guys okay?"

"Yup," I said smoothly, shifting in my seat to ease the pressure on my groin. "Everything is fine. Evie was just getting all worked up, telling me how passionately she feels about the new lingerie line. Evie, why don't you tell Cullen what you were saying to me?"

Evie lifted her chin and nodded. "Sure, yeah. I was saying how the new line is old school and vintage-looking but with a modern twist. Really fine laces with pearl buttons, but instead of the standard black and cream, we've added all those luscious new colors. In fact," she sent a vicious smile my way, "I've already snagged a bra-and-panty set in every color. The raspberry is my favorite."

Ungh.

The raspberry would look so good on her golden skin. An image of her bent over the desk in front of me wearing only a pair of raspberry lace panties sent a pulse of electricity straight to my dick.

She looked so triumphant, there was no need to wonder if she knew how deftly she'd scored.

Evie—one. Smith—zero.

"I'm really glad to hear you guys are so into the business talk. Because that's actually why I asked you both here today. I have some amazing news," Cullen said, giving each of us a meaningful look.

Evie shot me a worried glance and I shrugged, equally as confused as she was. I had no clue what the big news was, unless he hadn't told her about my investing and taking on a temporary position in the company yet?

"We are officially going to be a team. The three amigos!" Cullen beamed at us both, waiting for us to join in on the excitement, but we sat there frozen in stony silence.

I found my voice first and straightened my tie, trying to act casual. "When you say 'team,' what exactly do you mean?"

Evie didn't work at the company. Sure, she had a stake like all of her family did, but she didn't have any dealings in the day-to-day running of the company. She'd just graduated from college and was supposed to be traveling to find herself, or whatever recent college grads did.

"Evie decided to take the position I offered her in marketing. She'll be handling our social media presence. You yourself said it was a soft point for us, Smith."

I squeezed my eyes closed for a moment, wishing I had a fucking time machine to go back and punch my past self in the face for saying that.

"And I've got new office space that will accommodate us all back in Chicago, ready and waiting," Cullen continued.

"I'm sorry, but doesn't Smith already have a job?" Evie's voice was shrill and slightly panicked as she drummed her fingers restlessly against her thigh.

"He does. But mostly consulting work now, and investments. He offered me six months of his time and expertise, and I'd be a fool not to take it." Cullen sat back in his chair with a satisfied smile. "It's going to be great. The three of us together are going to take this business from the red back into the black in no time."

The room went quiet as the ramifications of what he was saying sank in.

"What's wrong? Why are you two acting so weird?"

Cullen asked with a frown.

No matter how much I'd teased Evie, the last thing I wanted was for Cullen to sense what had happened between us and that things had shifted.

I pasted on a smile and shook my head. "Nothing wrong here. Just took me by surprise, is all. When we crunched the numbers last night, I didn't see her salary as a line item."

"Yeah, I was still working through that, so I just plugged in a marketing consultant with a flat rate, remember?"

Now that he mentioned it, I did remember. Damn me for not asking more questions.

"Evie, this cool with you?" Cullen asked, turning toward his sister.

"Of course," she said with a snort. "Super cool. Like, so cool, the coolest."

She was babbling. And Evie never babbled.

Cullen let out a confused chuckle and rubbed his hands together. "Glad to hear it. So, I just got a call about the new line from the distributor. What say we get to work?"

My mind was still reeling as he chattered on, pulling out swatches and advertising mock-ups from his bag. I'd managed to keep my cool about what happened in my hotel room and joke around with her about it because it was fleeting. A moment in time. One I'd look back on and fondly remember. And sure, I'd have to see her for a few days while we were in Paris, but then? It would be back to seeing her at the occasional holiday party.

Now? Seeing Evie all day, every day?

I sure as hell wasn't laughing anymore. This woman was going to be the death of me.

Chapter Seven

Evie

Could this Monday suck any harder?

Scrubbing at the coffee stain on my cream silk blouse with a wet wipe, I muttered a curse under my breath. Today should have been a super-exciting one—after four years of busting my ass in college, it was my first day of work at my first job, finally contributing in a meaningful way. I would be embracing my spot in the family empire, as the right hand to my brother who was at the helm.

Instead I'd just spent fifteen minutes looking for the freaking door to this mammoth building, having to walk all the way around the block twice.

Who can't find a door? Me, apparently.

After stuffing the wipes back into my oversized purse, I sipped the now cooled coffee where it had pooled after overflowing on the mouthpiece of the lid.

I pulled open the glass door to our suite and spotted my brother straight away. The office was hardly more than a large open room—complete with a concrete floor and exposed ductwork overhead. Cullen had told me it was nothing fancy, but this was bare bones.

"Did you find it okay?" my brother asked, glancing up from his laptop with a smile.

I shot a death glare his way.

He chuckled under his breath. "Sorry, I meant to tell you. It's weird right now with the remodel going on. You have to enter where it says Billy's Bagels and then go up one flight of stairs." He waved his hand. "Never mind. You obviously figured it out. You're here."

Smith wasn't here yet. At least I'd beat him here, and I could take a moment to get my bearings.

"I would give you a tour, but—" Cullen gestured to the office around us. "This is it. Copy room's over there. Bathrooms are down the hall."

The room was large, and one entire wall was windows that provided a view of a construction site below. It was basic, but had a certain charm to it.

In many ways, we were still functioning as a start-up

company. We didn't need anything fancy. When my brother took over a couple of years ago, the company was barely turning a profit, just enough for him to survive on. Now it was poised to do a couple million in sales this year—if we could get our inventory issues sorted out, and the big accounts came through on their promised orders. It was an exciting time for everyone.

"You'll be right here. Between me and Smith." Cullen gestured to a center desk wedged between two others.

They weren't large or glamorous, but still they were nice—white Formica with chrome legs, and white leather swivel chairs. A gray rug cushioned the concrete floor beneath our feet, and a little steel trash can was tucked beneath each of the three desks. On top of each desk, a bright orange pencil holder sat next to a laptop computer. It felt organized and neat, and I liked that.

There was also a large work table under the windows on which sat piles of bras, camisoles, and books and books of fabric swatches.

"Thanks, Cullen. For believing in me." I smiled as I lowered myself into my seat next to him.

"Of course, sis." He returned my easy smile. "If you want to start by getting set up on our network, I e-mailed you the instructions."

"Network?" I took another sip of my coffee.

"Yeah, so we all have access to shared files and company documents. And it gives you access to the fax machine and printer." He tipped his head toward the back corner of the room, where a doorway led to a little copy room.

"Cool. I can't wait to dig in and get to work."

But just then my mojo was thrown off when Smith walked in, looking so strikingly sexy in his suit that I almost swallowed my tongue.

"Suit and tie . . . You didn't need to bother," Cullen said as Smith approached.

Cullen was dressed in jeans and a T-shirt, just as he was most days. Come to think of it, I'd never really seen Smith out of his suit. He wore it like a knight wore his armor, almost as if it had the power to shield him from the world.

"Morning," Smith rasped out in his husky morning voice, and my entire body took notice.

Shrugging off the strap of his laptop bag, he lowered himself into the seat next to mine. Close enough that I could smell his crisp masculine scent. This should have been the most exciting time of my adult life, but instead it was marred by the fact that I'd had a failed, awkward one-night stand with my brother's bestie, his business partner, and my new coworker.

This was like some sick joke. How would I survive sitting a few feet away from Smith for nine hours a day? Fuck my life. If I could quit, I would.

Cullen and Smith launched into a conversation about fourth-quarter purchase orders and gross revenue projections that I mostly ignored while I tried not to hyperventilate.

I didn't just need this job. I *wanted* it so badly, my chest ached. I wanted desperately to prove to my parents and my brother that I could handle the real world and not fuck it up. I was born into wealth and privilege— loved and cherished, educated at the best schools. Now was my chance to finally prove that I was more than my privileged upbringing would suggest. I was ready to contribute. To get this weight off my shoulders that all I'd done my entire life so far was take.

Focusing my attention on the instructions in my e-mail, I soon had my laptop configured to the network. I opened a folder containing the company graphics and logo that a graphic designer had recently finished for us. I planned to spend the day updating our social media accounts with our new look, and then reaching out to some media accounts in the hopes that we could get press coverage.

I opened a new e-mail and attached the logo—*Sophia's* written in a pretty script font in a soft pink color overlaid on the transparent image of a lace bra—and typed out a brief message.

Maggie,

Check out our new logo. Super cute, right? Oh, and I'm sitting three feet from Smith. Can you say torture?

I typed in her name and clicked ENTER, then SEND. It was only after I hit SEND that I noticed the e-mail address field said *Mack*, not Maggie.

"Um . . . who's Mack Lively?" I asked, reading over the address in my sent box.

Cullen swallowed, turning toward me. "He's the head of the regional department store chain out of Boston we're hoping to land. Why?"

My stomach bottomed out, and the coffee I'd consumed might as well have been battery acid for how sick I suddenly felt.

"I accidentally sent him an e-mail meant for Maggie."

"Shit, Evie. How did that happen?"

I released a slow exhale. The beginnings of a splitting headache set in. I'd been at work a mere thirty minutes and I'd already fucked up. I blamed Smith's presence—he had me agitated, but it wasn't like I could tell Cullen that.

"I started typing in M-A, and then I hit ENTER. Maggie's name normally auto-populates. I don't even have this Mack person's e-mail address. I don't understand."

Cullen swore under his breath, and Smith's somber expression looked like he felt sorry for me.

"You're connected to the network, Evie," Cullen said. "You have access to all the clients and contacts now." He released a sigh through his nose, his jaw tense.

"Right. I'm sorry. It won't happen again."

"What was in the e-mail?" Cullen asked, his expression darkening.

"Just our new logo . . . and some other stuff." I looked down at my keyboard, my mood plummeting even further.

Smith cleared his throat. "It's first-day nerves. A simple mistake that anyone could have made. I'm sure it's nothing to worry about. Don't sweat it, Evie."

I released the breath I was holding.

Cullen nodded. "Don't put too much pressure on yourself; it's day one. You'll learn the ropes soon enough."

I tried to smile and took another sip of my coffee. At least he didn't suspect that the hulking six-foot-something man beside us was the real reason for my nerves.

• • •

Somehow, I survived my first day. After my disastrous morning, I kept my head down and my eyes on my screen, speaking only in one-word responses to Smith and Cullen, afraid I would somehow out myself.

Smith's playful mood from Paris had evaporated, and he'd spent the day brooding and despondent. I wasn't cut out for this level of torture, which made me extremely thankful when I saw Maggie enter the bar after work.

"Thank God you're here," I mumbled, curling my fingers around the stem of my wineglass.

Maggie flashed me a gloomy frown. "Hey, sweetie. You're going to need something stronger than that." She tipped her chin toward my glass of merlot.

I shrugged. It didn't matter. Alcohol wasn't going to solve this.

I'd told Maggie the entire sordid tale when I got back from Paris. To her credit, she'd only laughed once at my ridiculous plan to break into Smith's hotel room, and then winced when I told her how he'd pulled away and practically kicked me out as soon as he realized it was me.

Since then, she'd offered sympathetic support and gentle encouragement.

Her stance? It was time to move on. And didn't I know it. I just wished there was a way to erase the past. What I needed was a time machine.

"It was torturous. He's sitting so close that I can smell his cologne. And he looks at me like he feels bad for me."

Maggie nodded. "That's exactly why I have the perfect new plan for you."

"I'm all ears," I said, then drained the last of my wine and signaled the bartender for another glass.

"The best way to get over someone is to get under someone else."

Emboldened by the alcohol, we created a new plan— an online dating profile that Maggie typed up for me on my phone.

"Ms. Fifty Shades of Sexy seeks lovable Christian Grey type for cuddling, misadventure, and more."

I snatched my phone back from her. "You can't write

that."

She smiled like the cat who'd eaten the canary. "Oops. Too late."

By the time we'd polished off a bottle of wine and eaten a few tacos apiece from a food truck out front, I felt immensely better. On the cab ride home, anything seemed possible.

Maybe I wouldn't die a pathetic spinster with a cobwebbed vagina after all. I had a new plan, one that had nothing to do with Smith Hamilton. It didn't matter that I'd been in love with him half my life . . . it was more than past time to move on.

My failed attempt at seducing him was like a flashing neon sign from God to move on. *Smith who?*

Tomorrow was a new day.

Chapter Eight

Smith

I stared at my computer screen. For the tenth time that day, I saw not a single number in front of me, in spite of the fact that they filled the screen from top to bottom.

Nope, instead of eights, I saw the lush curves of one Evie Reed in all her glory, sprawled on my hotel bed.

Instead of sixes and nines, my brain instantly supplied a dozen carnal images of the two of us doing exactly that. My mouth on that sweet, wet pussy, and her hot, juicy lips wrapped around my cock.

Instead of ones, I recalled the secret knowledge that I was the only man to have been inside her.

It had been a week since we'd left France to head back to the States and begun working together on a daily basis. I wasn't an idiot—I'd known day one would be bad. And I was right. Monday had been the ultimate shit show, with the two of us steering around each other awkwardly like ships passing in the night.

Except I wanted to fuck this particular ship so badly, I was in a near-constant state of arousal.

By the time Tuesday had rolled around, I figured I had it on lock. I'd jerked off when I got home Monday night, and then again before I left for the office the next morning.

Then Evie had decided Tuesday was apparently the appropriate time to roll out a brand-new pair of black fuck-me pumps, complete with freshly painted scarlet toes peeking out, and I was a goner.

I got through the day, but barely.

Cue Wednesday, when I had not only rubbed one out in the shower before work, but had also removed myself from the premises to work at the coffee shop downstairs, decreeing to all who would listen that I was doing something super number-y and super important, and was not to be disturbed. The truth was I just couldn't make it another second in her presence without doing or saying something inappropriate.

I'd made it to two in the afternoon without incident, until I had no choice but to venture out for a late lunch. It was like fate was working against me, because I stepped into the building's lobby and directly into Evie's path. She skidded to a halt, but not before her soft breasts bounced off my bicep and the papers she'd been holding went fluttering everywhere.

I spent a full minute picking up the scattered sheets with her pert little pencil-skirt-covered ass mere inches from my face. I'd handed the papers over only to catch a whiff of her light, citrusy scent, and it was Stiffy Central all over again.

Flash forward to today. Friday, the start of the weekend.

Instead of planning some great activity—maybe a wine tasting, a dinner date, or a hike—I was prepping for a whack-a-thon. Cueing up enough porn on my laptop to fill my days and nights in hopes of coming into next week with the old tank on empty. I was a thirty-year-old man, but felt like I was sixteen all over again.

I blew out a sigh and glanced at the clock. *Five fifteen.* I'd built in the extra quarter of an hour so as not to get stuck riding in the elevator alone with Evie, and it was finally time to go.

I packed up my briefcase and snagged the file I'd barely gotten anything done on due to my distraction, vowing to catch up over the weekend. With one last glance at my desk to be sure I hadn't forgotten anything, I swept out of the office and down the hall.

"Hey. No overtime on a Friday," Evie murmured in a low voice as she stepped up beside me with a smile.

She matched her stride to mine as we walked toward the elevators, and it was all I could do not to turn and snarl at her like a cornered dog. Did she have any idea what she was doing to me?

I shot a glance her way only because I couldn't seem to help myself, and swallowed a groan. She'd clearly made plans for after work, because in place of the fitted blazer she'd worn to the office that morning, she had on a peach cashmere sweater. It hung saucily off one shoulder, revealing about five inches of creamy skin that I wanted to lick more than I wanted to take my next breath.

Her glossy peach-colored lips were tipped up in a smile as she cocked her head. "You okay? You look . . . weird," she said, her brow furrowing.

I had to bite back a bark of laughter at that. *Weird, you mean like all I can think about is fucking-your-brains-out weird?*

But what I actually said was, "Nah. Just been a long week. Ready to get out and get the weekend started."

We slowed in unison in front of the elevators and both reached for the DOWN button at the same time. Our fingers brushed, and she jerked back like I'd burned her.

"Sorry," she squeaked. "Go ahead."

I punched the arrow and then shot her another quick look. I should have resisted the urge, because what I saw only made my struggles that much worse. All week long, I'd been caught up in my own misery. On the occasions I hadn't been able to avoid seeing her face-to-face, Evie had seemed like she'd gotten past what had happened between us in Paris. But now, watching as a flush stained her cheeks and her pupils dilated, I wasn't so sure.

It was one thing for me to manage my own desire. It hadn't been easy, but I was getting by, albeit pathetically.

Now, though? Seeing that look on her face and realizing that, just maybe, she still wanted me too? Hard didn't even come close to describing it.

My cock took on a life of its own. Swelling and thickening in my pants like an entity entirely separate from my body.

We both stood stock-still as we waited for what felt like a year until the elevator dinged. When the doors finally opened, I waved her in, catching a glimpse of hard nipples poking against that cashmere sweater. My throat went dry as I stepped in beside her, making sure to keep a solid two feet between us.

The second the door closed, the tension grew even thicker.

People fucked in elevators all the time. Not just in porn or in movies, but in real life too. In my mind, Evie took one big step forward, smashed her hand over that red STOP button, and then walked right up to me. She crushed her lithe body against mine, covered my cock with her hand, and said, "Take me, Smith. Fuck me until I scream."

In real life, though, none of that happened. We stood there with only our combined labored breaths filling the tiny space until *finally*, the torture box stopped moving.

God damn it, this is frustrating.

When the doors slid open, we both practically dived out of the elevator and mumbled quick good-byes. It wasn't until an hour later, behind closed doors and the safety of my apartment, that I finally got some relief from the agony she was putting me through.

I stood in the shower, water rolling off me as I gritted my teeth, my cock in hand. I could have blown in two strokes, I was so hard and wanting. Instead, I drew it out, imagining Evie was in the stall with me. On her knees, droplets of water shimmering on her naked flesh as she sucked me. That long honey-colored hair wet beneath my hands as I used it to work her over my shaft. Slow and easy at first, then long and deep. Until the head of my cock butted against the back of her throat.

My dream Evie didn't pull away. She pulled me closer, murmuring encouragement, taking me deeper. She rose up higher on her knees, and her slick, wet breasts grazed my thighs as she bobbed rhythmically up and down.

"Ah, fuck," I groaned.

I was coming. I could feel the hot liquid pooling in my balls, making them achy and heavy. One more firm stroke, and then it was over. I jerked, my legs quaking as every nerve ending came to life in a rush. Hot cum jetted out onto the dripping tiles, painting them glossy white as I sucked in a shuddering breath.

I braced myself against the wall as I came down, slowly returning to the cold reality of the situation.

I was alone in my shower, and while that had been an oh-so-necessary release, it didn't even put a dent into the perverse thoughts I was still having about Evie. It had been nothing more than a bodily function, like eating or sleeping. My dick knew what it wanted, and it was already perking back to life as images of her floated back into my mind.

"God damn it," I muttered, shoving away from the wall in frustration.

I washed up and hosed off the tile before stepping out of the shower, filled with a restless energy I couldn't control. If I didn't get a handle on this, it wasn't just my own comfort and sanity at stake. Soon enough, Cullen was going to get his head out of his ass long enough to see what was right in front of him. There had to be a way for Evie and me to act normal in front of him, and I needed to figure out how to do that, and fast.

I was just shoving my legs into a pair of gym pants to go for a run when my cell phone chirped to life.

PAM: Hey, bro. Dinner tomorrow, turkey and all the fixings. Five o'clock. Be there or be square. And don't mention Winnie's missing tooth. She's feeling sensitive about it.

In spite of my black mood, the text from my older sister made me grin, and I tapped out a quick reply.

SMITH: I'll be there. And don't worry, I'll make sure not to mention the kid's tooth.

I set the phone down as I slid on my sneakers and laced up.

Maybe I'd been going about this whole Evie thing all

wrong. Maybe instead of being alone like some sort of hermit, I needed to get out and be around people I cared about. Once old Uncle Smith played tea party and was ridden like a pony for a few hours, surely he'd stop thinking about Evie.

That decided, I set out for my run. I wouldn't come back until my legs shook with fatigue. Then I'd get a good night's sleep and head out to the mall to buy some toys for my niece and nephews, and leave all thoughts of Evie Reed deep down the drain of my shower stall, where they belonged.

• • •

"You look ridiculuth," she stated flatly.

I fixed a hurt expression on my face as I popped a squat to get eye level with my niece, Winnie. "That's a little harsh. I think I look pretty good. Besides, I got lots of loot from the tooth fairy for this, so if I have to look silly for a while, I can handle it."

Winnie propped a hand on one hip and eyed my blacked-out front tooth that mirrored her own newly emancipated one, her cherubic face screwed up in suspicion. For a second, I was sure she was going to reach out and scratch at it, and I'd be busted.

Instead, she asked, "What did you get from the tooth fairy?"

"Loads of stuff," I said with a grin. "A new video game and a remote control car, some cookies and—"

"All I got wath a dollar," she said mournfully.

"Funny you should mention that." I stood and pulled a wrapped package from behind my back. "The tooth fairy left this mixed in with my packages. I wonder if she forgot to leave it when you lost your tooth the other night?"

Winnie's chubby cheeks widened into a smile, showcasing one deep dimple that made my heart melt a little every time I saw it.

"For me?"

She was only five, but she was wicked smart. Smart enough to know every word I'd said was a lie, but opting to go along with it anyway because . . . *presents*.

I nodded. "Yup."

She squealed and tore into the package like a starving rottweiler into a rotisserie chicken.

"Hello, darling brother. You just won't be happy unless she's spoiled rotten, will you?" my sister Pam asked, rolling her eyes as she padded barefoot down the hall toward me.

Her youngest, Mac, was parked on her hip in his preferred spot, and she wiped her free hand on her Wicked Witch of the West apron before pulling me into a one-armed hug.

"It's been too long, brother mine," she murmured.

The scent of fresh-baked bread filled my nose as I nodded in agreement, hugging her back.

"I had that work trip and started the new job working for Cullen, so time has been scarce. But I'll be around more now, so I won't miss Saturday dinner again for a while."

She punched me lightly on the shoulder and tucked a long lock of brown hair behind her ear. She looked every bit a flower-child, go-with-the-flow hippie, but also ran a successful bakery. With three kids, a dog, and a husband who was a great guy but rather like a big kid himself at times, she truly was a marvel.

It was only now, as I looked closer, that I noted the dark circles under her eyes, and concern pricked at me hard. She was usually like Wonder Woman, with boundless energy that helped her manage on five hours of sleep, no sweat.

"What's up? Everything okay with you and Tim?" I asked gently.

"Yeah, he's great."

Her smile was strained, and my concern expanded into a sharp jab of fear.

"You're not sick, are you, Pammie?"

She shook her head and patted Winnie's head absently as she admired the gift the "tooth fairy" had brought her daughter.

"Healthy as a horse, unless you consider morning sickness an illness," she muttered for my ears only.

I stared at her pale face and threw back my head and laughed, relief coalescing with excitement.

"Are you fu—freaking kidding me?" I demanded, pulling her in for another squeeze. "Was this the plan or what?"

Her semi-hysterical laugh told me more than words could, but as I looked harder, I could see the shine in her eyes.

"We're excited. It's just a shock, is all. We have a lot to work out as far as trying to juggle everything. I know in the long run, it will be great, but I'm a little terrified right now," she admitted, taking my arm and drawing me into the kitchen. The room was warm and cozy like the rest of the house, and smelled like roasting meat and sweet rolls.

"Tim, Finn! Uncle Smith is here. Come down and let's eat!" she called up the back stairs.

Whoops and hollers rang out as my other nephew pattered down the stairs in a rush to launch his little body at me with glee.

This was good. Exactly what the doctor ordered. In fact, I didn't think about Evie for a whole forty-five minutes as the adults shared a bottle of wine and the kids slipped their peas under the table for Salvador Doggy, their constantly hungry dachshund.

By the time dessert came, I was feeling confident and in charge. Yeah, so Evie and I had rolled around a bit. Big deal. It was just the unusual circumstance of wanting and not being able to have that had me all hung up. So long as I kept myself busy, I'd be fine.

But when a luscious strawberry shortcake hit the table, piled high with mounds of decadent whipped cream, my mind went instant caveman.

Evie, stretched out on this very table, buck naked, whipped cream on both tits and at the juncture of her thighs, her lips parted and her eyes gleaming as she waits for me to come and get it.

Jesus, was I fucked. I squeezed my eyes closed in defeat.

Operation: Whack-A-Thon had failed.

Operation: Keep Myself Busy so I Can Keep My Mind off Her had failed.

That left only one option . . .

Operation: Get Evie Naked Again and Fuck Her Brains out so We Can Both Move On was now in full effect.

My cock bucked in agreement, and as I dug my fork into my shortcake, I began to plot my first move.

Chapter Nine

Evie

Back at work on Monday, I was feeling positive. I'd set up my dating profile and already had an in-box full of potential new suitors. Not that I was interested in any of them. But just having them there—just knowing that option was on the table—gave me a little boost to my step.

"Hey, sis."

"Hi, guys." I slid into my seat between them, opened my laptop, and kept my eyes on the screen as it loaded, knowing if I looked at Smith, my positive mood would die a quick death.

"Morning, Everleigh." Smith's rich voice rolled over every syllable in my name and washed over me like a wave.

Tempted, I sneaked a look at the man next to me. Dressed in a white dress shirt and a navy tie, he looked deliciously preppy, like he could grace the cover of a men's clothing catalog. The dark stubble dusting his square jaw only added to the appeal. His gaze moved over me, a question in his expression that I couldn't quite read.

Are you okay? it seemed to say.

No, that wasn't it.

Are we okay?

Meeting his eyes with their flecks of gold and green and amber, I gave him a quick nod. Even if things were weird as hell right now, this was still Smith. Of course we'd be okay. We had to be.

My brother spoke, interrupting the intense eye contact Smith and I were sharing. "I have a call with the manufacturer this morning. Depending on what they say about their capacity, it could change some of the fourth-quarter plans we've made. I'll keep you both posted."

"Sounds good, buddy," Smith said.

I opened my e-mail and saw a response from the consultant I'd been in touch with about helping increase our social engagement. I was typing out a response when Cullen answered his cell and rose to his feet. He wondered toward the wall of windows, pacing as he spoke.

Smith turned to face me. "Can I talk to you for a second?"

"Of course."

"About . . . *things*."

My gaze wondered over toward my brother. He was absorbed in his conversation, but that didn't mean he wouldn't overhear what was sure to be a rather personal conversation.

"Not here," I whispered.

"Have lunch with me today."

My gaze left his and wandered back to my screen. I wasn't so sure that was a good idea, and Smith seemed to read my mind.

"You owe me at least a conversation, don't you think?"

"Fine." I took a deep breath, already anticipating that the hours until lunch would now drag by at a snail's pace.

My brother conveniently took off for the gym just before noon, meaning Smith and I wouldn't have to sneak out to lunch together. For that, I was relieved.

Fifteen minutes later, Smith pulled out my chair and waited until I sat down in front of the sushi bar before lowering his tall frame into the seat beside me. After we placed an order for iced tea and three types of sushi rolls, Smith turned to face me.

"Thanks for joining me. I think we need to discuss this like two rational adults."

I lifted the bamboo chopsticks from their resting place beside my plate and shook my head. "There's nothing to discuss."

"Let's agree to disagree." He leaned in closer, his voice dropping lower. "There was a reason you climbed into my bed that night, and I'd like to know what that reason was."

I glanced at the businessmen seated beside us. Could we have picked a less private spot to have this conversation? All the tables had already been taken at the popular Japanese restaurant Smith had chosen, leaving us to wedge ourselves in at the last two open seats at the sushi bar.

"I'm not discussing this in public," I all but hissed.

Smith inhaled through his nostrils, his posture tensing. "Fine. My place, tonight. We'll have dinner and figure out where to go from here."

"I'm busy tonight," I lied.

"Tomorrow then."

I shook my head. "I'm busy all week."

I wasn't, but I would find something to do. Between Maggie and the gym, I'd invent reasons to stay far, far away from Smith's apartment.

"Perfect. Friday night, then."

I rolled my eyes. "Why are you doing this? You want to be my white knight, rescue me from the memory of that horrible night?"

"I never said it was horrible."

Hope bloomed in my chest, but before I could respond, the server delivered a platter with rolls of spicy tuna, eel, and cucumber rolls.

"We'll figure everything out this Friday," Smith

added. "Now, dig in. I know how crabby you get when you're hungry."

He shot me a smile, and for the first time since all this started, I felt at ease.

• • •

"Tell me this is a terrible idea," I begged Maggie before taking a sip of chardonnay.

I'd weighed the pros and cons all week, and now it was Thursday night, meaning that I was out of time. Tomorrow I'd be expected to spend the evening with Smith. Unless my best friend could help me figure a way out of this.

"Meh." She lifted one shoulder, munching on a pretzel as we sat at the breakfast bar at my apartment.

While it was true I'd wanted to be intimate with Smith for my real first time, now I wasn't so sure.

"What exactly did he say again?" Maggie asked.

I waved a hand at her. "Let's talk about something else. Literally *anything* else," I begged.

"Fine." She grabbed another handful of pretzels, picking the chunks of crystallized salt off each one with her fingernail. "Sam and I are going to try that new nightclub tomorrow. I might need to raid your closet later."

I had to share Maggie with Sam, the male counterpart to me. He and I often joked that we had joint custody of her. They'd grown up as best friends, and despite him having a penis, they'd never drifted apart or let things get awkward between them, even when they both started dating other people.

"You're welcome to anything in my closet. You know that." My clothes were tame compared to hers.

"The place is pretty risqué, so I was actually thinking maybe just a bustier and a miniskirt. Or would that be too skanky?"

I pursed my lips. I wouldn't have the balls to pull it off, but hey, if Maggie was brave enough to venture out in little more than her underwear, more power to her.

"Actually, our new Lovely Lace collection has a really pretty bustier," I said. "That might be perfect."

I wasn't brave enough to wear something like that, or maybe it was just that I didn't have a man to wear it for. And the naive hope that Smith would be the man to change all that had all but died inside me.

Chapter Ten

Smith

Mirepoix.

I stared down at the cookbook with a scowl and reached for the laptop on the counter a few feet away. It only took a second to look up the term once I got the spelling right.

Carrots, celery, and onion.

Right.

This was exactly why I didn't cook, aside from burgers and steaks on the grill most of the time. These chefs had to use fancy words for simple things, and I was pretty sure that was by design just to make guys like me feel stupid.

I'd made the mistake of asking my sister Pam what I could make for a woman I was having over for dinner.

"Well, that depends," Pam had said. "Do you want to impress her?"

I'd stupidly answered yes. Then I did some backpedaling, framing all of this in a hypothetical fashion, since there was no way in fuck I was going to admit to my sister that I was courting Evie fucking Reed.

Pam had laughed and said, "Well, hypothetically speaking, I would make this," and then she shoved the French cookbook at me, the page for the recipe dog-eared.

I made my way over to the fridge and pulled out the ingredients for my *mirepoix* and brought it back to the cutting board. All the while, a voice in my head kept telling me I was being a chump for feeling like a teenager getting ready for the freaking prom.

This wasn't even a date. Not really, anyway. This was me trying to be an adult about the searing-hot attraction between Evie and me. And so, yeah, we were going to stuff some food into our faces while we talked about it.

Not even a date.

But you did buy that bottle of wine. And you did vacuum the living room for the first time in like five months.

"Ah, shut up," I muttered to the voice inside my

head.

It wasn't a date, and that was that. And under no circumstances was this night going to end with any part of me inside any part of Evie. That much I'd vowed to myself already. She and Cullen were super close. Cullen and I were almost as close as that. No way in hell was I going to become the wedge that tore us all apart. The Reed family business would suffer, and we'd all wind up losing something way more valuable than just sex . . .

No matter how hot it was.

My cock swelled at the thought and I ruthlessly shut it down, calling up an image of my ninth-grade gym teacher, Mr. Tubolowski. I'd walked in on him once when he was changing and had caught him buck naked. He was hung like a Clydesdale, his balls nearly scraping the floor, and perpetually smelled of gym shoes and hot garbage. If that mental image didn't kill this boner, nothing would.

"Mirepoix," I muttered under my breath, chopping carrots and trying to avoid my fingers. Apparently, they looked just like carrots, because I wound up nicking one and slicing a flap of skin off another, and had to start all over again after disinfecting and taping up.

As I finished up the slicing, dicing, and dismemberment portion of my show, I realized with a start that it had been years since I'd cooked for a woman. Sure, I'd bring along some sour cream dip or hot wings to a Sunday football viewing, but mostly, I was the guy who came in with a bucket of something fried.

In fact, I was pretty sure I hadn't done it since Karen and I had split over four years ago. I used to cook Sunday morning breakfast for the two of us, but when things went south, that had stopped, right along with just about anything else fun. Once she realized I wasn't going to marry her, she'd shut down completely.

Who could blame her, though? She'd put in two years of her life, and no matter how much my mind tried to convince me that it all made sense on paper, my heart wouldn't listen. I just couldn't bring myself to pull the trigger.

Now, looking back as I anticipated this evening with Evie, I realized it had never felt ... easy enough with Karen. I cared for her deeply and she was a good person, and the sex was frequent and solid. It was just that I never felt like I was truly myself around her.

Probably my own fault, but there it was.

I set the vegetables into a frying pan with some olive oil to sauté and then took out the roasting chicken, but my mind wasn't on fowl. It was on Evie. Exactly where it had been since that night in Paris.

Tonight, we'd spend some time together. Simply because I wanted to, not just because I wanted to figure out what was happening between us. I was exactly where I wanted to be, doing exactly what I wanted to be doing right now.

Bandages, mirepoix, blue-ball misery, and all. I wouldn't change a thing.

The realization gave me pause, but for once, I didn't fight it. The Reed family had been one of the only real constants in my life. Yeah, my adoptive family was amazing. And my siblings, especially Pam and my brother Dave, had filled a huge hole created by being abandoned and in foster care.

But my siblings were sort of stuck with me. I wasn't going anywhere. The Reeds, however, had chosen me.

Cullen had wanted to be my friend even when I was

the new kid at school who had just appeared one day as part of the Hamilton clan. Evie had accepted me just as quickly, treating me like an older brother through my teen years and into my early twenties.

Somewhere along the line, those feelings had clearly changed on her part. And now I realized they'd been changing on mine as well.

But at the core of it, as uncomfortable as the past couple of weeks had been, working with them day to day and spending time with Evie felt . . . right.

So, for the time being, I was going to roll with it. Not question my every move, not wonder how it could all crash and burn. I was going to enjoy Evie's company, and take things from there.

And you're sure we can't fuck her? my cock asked with a wiggle behind my zipper.

"I'm sure," I muttered under my breath.

• • •

An hour later, my house smelled like Emeril Lagasse had stopped by, and I was fucking stoked. The scent of roasting meat and caramelized onions and garlic filled the air, making my mouth water. I couldn't wait for Evie to try it. Hell, I couldn't wait for her to walk through the door, to see her face, to talk and laugh and drink with her. I didn't realize how much I missed having someone else around this place until now.

With a jolt, I wondered if this weird feeling I'd been having might just be sheer loneliness. I'd settled into an easy, no-risk routine of sex for the sake of it, and some casual dates. All the while, I'd avoided addressing this vague sense of dissatisfaction that never really left. Whenever I saw a new movie trailer or had some great news about work, there was no one to tell. And damned if it hadn't been weighing on me.

Until now. Because right now, I couldn't wait to spend my evening talking to Evie about all those things.

I shot a quick glance at the clock and realized she'd be here soon. I was just about to start on the salad when my cell phone buzzed.

CULLEN: *Wanna go out for a couple beers?*

I stared at the screen for a long moment, my gut tightening a little.

Shit, Cullen. He'd asked me before I left work what I was doing this weekend, and I'd already said I was keeping it low key. He'd been elbow deep in new ad concepts and told me he planned to stay until he was done, so it never occurred to me that he'd get in touch tonight to hang out.

I paused with my thumb hovering over the keys as I tried to craft a response. I didn't want to lie. It was already giving me heartburn having to even lie by omission. Bullshitting him straight up would kill me.

I tapped out five different replies before I finally hit SEND.

SMITH: *Can't, man. Put together some last-minute dinner plans.*

Vague. True. It checked all the boxes, and hopefully that would be the end of—

CULLEN: Nice! Do I know her? And if not, will I get to meet her? Been a while since you brought a girl home.

Fuck.

A direct question. No ... two direct questions, neither of which I could answer without dragging this on and on until I just told him the truth.

Not an option.

My mood soured instantly as all the anticipation I'd been feeling about seeing Evie cooled under the guilt of having to lie to my best friend and her brother.

SMITH: She's an old friend who recently reconnected. Beers, maybe Sunday?

I silenced my phone and tossed it on the kitchen table with a clatter, feeling as crummy as the gum stuck on the bottom of a shoe.

Some friend I was. One second, mentally waxing poetic about the bond Cullen and I had and how great of a guy he was, and the next, lying through my teeth about his sister.

I turned my attention back to the salad, but I couldn't bring myself to care about it anymore. Before, I'd been so proud of the meal and psyched to share it with Evie. Now I had this black cloud hanging over my head, and no way to shake it. As rosy as I'd been painting this picture not five minutes before, the fact was, we were sneaking around. Being deceptive and shady, and all the things I despised in a person.

I snatched up my phone, ignoring the response from Cullen as I tapped out a message to Evie. No matter what I did at this point, I was going to feel like shit, and having Evie over would only be miserable for us both. Better to cancel this now before we went any further with things.

I held the phone in my hand, dread tightening my chest. When the screen lit up again, I read Evie's reply and let out a groan.

> EVIE: *Who cancels three minutes before a date? I'm literally outside your apartment building, asshole.*

Who, indeed?

I stiffened my jaw and thumbed out a quick reply.

SMITH: Sorry. Come on up.

So I'd fucked up. Again. I'd get through tonight with Evie, make some excuse about thinking I needed stitches from my mirepoix injuries, and she would be fine.

Then tomorrow, things needed to go back to normal with her, because betraying a friend wasn't how I wanted to live my life.

But I couldn't quiet that annoying little voice inside my head that whispered, *Easier said than done.*

Chapter Eleven

Evie

This was not a date.

I pulled a deep breath into my lungs, refusing to let my lower lip tremble like it wanted to. I shouldn't be sad. I should be angry. And I was. But I was also confused. And hurt.

Smith was standing in the open doorway, a scowl painted on his features as he towered over me. His fingertips curled around the top of the doorframe above his head, and his T-shirt crept up an inch, flashing me a sliver of taut, muscled skin at his waistband.

"Hey," he said on a heavy exhale after several moments of silence.

He hadn't invited me in. Just stood there, watching me like he wasn't sure what to do with me.

"If my being here is an issue, I have no problem turning my ass around and going home." I had a pint of salted-caramel ice cream in my freezer, and the series I'd been bingeing on lately had just released a new season. "You asked me to come, remember?"

He dropped his hands to his sides, then shoved them into his pockets. "I don't want you to leave. Sorry about my text."

"What's going on, Smith?"

"Come inside. I'll explain."

He stepped back from the doorway and headed inside, assuming I'd follow. And of course, I did.

I hadn't been inside his apartment in a couple of years. The last time I'd been here had been when I was hanging out with my brother and we'd stopped by briefly. The place looked exactly as I remembered it—spacious for a Chicago apartment, neat and masculine. Buffed wood floors and dark wood furniture. Black-and-white photographs of his family and the city he loved hung on the walls.

Smith stopped in the dining room, placing his hands in his hair.

I should just leave now. Say *fuck this* and tell him to

take his silent treatment and shove it up his ass. But I knew I wouldn't do that.

I knew I'd said I just wanted to have one orgasm that wasn't supplied by me, but that wasn't exactly true. Because Smith *had* given me one. One amazing, earth-shattering, bed-clawing orgasm—with his mouth—and I still tingled at the memory, but now I wanted more. I wanted the full experience, and I was stubborn that way. Once I had it in my head that I wanted something, I didn't stop until I got it.

As I'd dressed and readied myself for my not-a-date, I couldn't help but let hope bloom in my chest. Knowing Smith, he probably wanted to razz me about my failed seduction attempt in person, just to watch my face flame and hear my voice tremble.

Well, fuck that. I wasn't going to beat myself up or turn into a babbling idiot when he asked me to explain myself tonight.

The fragrant scent of chicken and roasted vegetables came from the kitchen, making my stomach grumble.

He cooked?

"If you don't start talking soon, I'm out of here," I blurted.

My pride had already suffered too much where this man was concerned. I might have been kicked out of his bed once already, and if he didn't want me here, he wouldn't have to say anything. The moment I felt uncomfortable or unwelcome, I would say *peace, out* and hightail it out of here.

Chapter Twelve

Smith

"Please don't leave."

The words were out before I could stop them, despite the fact that I knew I should just let her go. No matter how much that might save my sanity, though, I couldn't stand seeing the hurt in Evie's eyes. I had invited her over. She'd done nothing to deserve my shitty attitude besides accept my invitation.

Not to mention she had clearly been anticipating this as much as I had before I got Cullen's texts, because she was dressed to the nines and looking dead sexy. Her black wrap dress accentuated every sleek curve, and my palms were itching to touch her.

She stared back at me, the indecision clear on her face. "You don't really seem to be in the mood for company . . ."

"I'm a dick sometimes. Surely we've known each other long enough that we can both admit it," I said with a sheepish grin. "But I promise," I held up three fingers in a solemn vow, "for the rest of the night, I'll be on my best behavior. So could you please stay? It would mean a lot to me."

I didn't realize how true those words were until she nodded slowly and a sense of relief washed over me.

"Okay. If you're sure."

"I am."

I wasn't. In fact, I was almost one hundred percent positive that this was the wrong move, long term. This whole struggle was only going to get worse. If things went great, I'd only want her more.

I had to bite back a laugh at the very idea that could even be possible. She was like sap on my skin, stuck tight, and there wasn't shit I could do to shake her except let whatever this was run its course. But if things went badly, the alternative wasn't any better.

In the face of her disappointment, though, I realized a few things. I cared about Evie, and I was going to make sure we enjoyed this night. Surely, tomorrow would be soon enough to rake myself over the fucking coals again.

"You forgive me for being such a jerk?" I asked softly.

She nodded and chewed on her bottom lip, which made me zero in on that mouth. Acting on instinct, I tugged her into my arms and held her tight against me for a long moment.

As she looped her arms around my neck and our bodies lined up, all I could think of was how right it felt. Like a key fitting into a lock. The last of the darkness faded away, and the loneliness that had become the norm for me lifted, leaving behind a happiness I hadn't felt in years. I had to fight the urge to clamp onto her even tighter and kiss her senseless. When she pressed closer to me, her breasts branding my chests as her nipples peaked, I guessed she must be feeling it too.

Fuck.

I clenched my jaw to hold back a groan as my dick pulsed to life and my blood ran hot. My fingers tightened almost reflexively, clamping over her waist, drawing a choked gasp from Evie that sent a pulse of electricity through me.

I pulled away first, fully aware that if I didn't do it now, I never would.

"I can't wait for you to try what I made for dinner," I said, praying to the boner gods to give me ten minutes of relief. "It's roasted chicken with skillet cornbread and stuffing."

Her cheeks were pink, and the hurt expression on her face had made way for a grin. "Sounds awesome."

I led her back into the dining room and motioned for her to take a seat. "You want to pour the wine while I get dinner on the table?"

"Will do."

I headed into the kitchen and prepped our plates. It only took a couple of minutes, but by the time I got back, the wine was poured and she'd moved some things around on the table.

"Okay, what's different?" I asked with a chuckle.

"Knives on the right," she said with a saucy wink. "And they call it a centerpiece for a reason. It goes in the middle. But I've got to tell you, Mr. Hamilton, I'm so impressed. All this for me?"

I shrugged and set down the plates. "Who better for than a friend I've known forever and care about, right?"

The light in her eyes dimmed a little as she took her seat again. "Exactly. Friends. And, um, thanks. It looks great."

For a smart guy, I could be such a fucking idiot sometimes. In my effort to make her feel special, I'd just decreed that this wasn't a date after all. It came out all wrong, and so far, my attempts at making tonight perfect were a major fail.

"Try the chicken," I said, hoping that maybe if the food was good enough, she'd forget about what an asshole I was.

She cut off a morsel and tucked it into her mouth. I didn't realize how important her reaction was until she made a low moan deep in her throat.

"Holy crap, that's good. So moist and juicy," she murmured.

A thrill shot through me, and I forked up a bite

myself just to make sure she wasn't bullshitting me. "You're right. Not bad, if I do say so myself. Pam gave me the recipe."

We worked our way around the plate, trying bites of everything at the same time and comparing notes. The meal went by without any more foot-in-mouth action, thank God, and when it was over, we were stuffed to the gills.

"How about I cook for you next time? I have this amazing lamb dish that—" She blinked and stopped short. "Not that there will be a next time, but . . ."

When she started toying with her napkin, I reached out and took her hand. "Evie, you don't have to tiptoe around me. I like spending time with you, and this was my idea, after all. I'd love to do it again."

She threaded her fingers with mine and held my gaze. "Then why did you try to break our date? And why were you in such a miserable mood at first? Did I do something wrong?"

I pushed my plate away with my free hand and leaned closer. It was time for a truth bomb. "Nope. Not a thing.

In fact, I was looking forward to it all day. Your brother texted me. He asked if I wanted to hang out tonight, and I had to lie. I hate lying to him."

Guilt clouded her eyes and she nodded slowly. "Me too. But what's the alternative? We can't hang out, or . . . maybe we could just tell him?"

I shook my head grimly. "We don't even know what this is yet, Evie. If we tell him and things never progress beyond what they are, then we've either got him pissed that I slept with his baby sister when that didn't even technically happen," *yet*, my brain supplied, "or he mentally marries us off when we both want this to be casual."

I didn't even know if I felt that way anymore. Casual was such a fleeting word. But, damn it, I couldn't deny that my heart was racing, and it wasn't just from anticipation at the thought of spending more time with Evie.

It was fear.

The thought of admitting my own loneliness—and the way Evie made me feel—scared the piss out of me.

Luckily for me, she didn't seem to notice, because she nodded in agreement.

"Casual. I'm in. And you're right. I hadn't thought of it that way, but we can't tell him. Ever. My brother can be overprotective and traditional like that. One sort-of date and he'll be asking when you're going to make an honest woman out of me. We've got to work together every day, and that kind of pressure will ruin any chance we have of juggling it all effectively."

"So, now I answered your question. We can't tell Cullen. Maybe you can finally answer mine," I said, tracing my thumb absently over her palm. "Why did you come in my room that night? Are you really so hung up on the virginity thing that you just wanted to get rid of it?"

"What?" she asked, suddenly blinking at me.

"I'm not doing this. I'm not going to be your first."

"You're not. I mean, you weren't," she said tentatively.

"Wait, what?" The knowledge there had been someone before me sent ice water through my veins. I wanted to kill the motherfucker, beat him within an inch of his life, and I didn't even know who the guy was.

"It was stupid. A guy I went out with last year. And it was horrible, as first times go."

A knot formed inside my gut. "Meaning what? You didn't enjoy yourself?"

Evie shook her head. "Not even a little. I wanted a do-over."

"A do-over?" That wasn't a thing. She knew that, right?

She shrugged. "My friend Maggie seemed to think it made sense."

There was no sense in explaining to Evie that you could only have your first time once. It was clear that she was set on her goal of having a satisfying sexual experience, and damn if I didn't respect the hell out of her for it.

She hesitated, but I could see her pulse jumping in her neck. "And I don't know. I thought it would be good . . . with *you*."

The tension in the air ratcheted up to the point that

her hand started trembling in mine, and my dick went stiff. I'd asked for it by posing the question, so I had no one to blame but myself.

"So you still want that? With me?"

She opened her mouth to speak and then closed it before tipping her head in the affirmative.

Blood rushed in my ears as I tried to get a grip. So, what Evie was saying was that, right now, if I wanted to sweep these plates off the table, hoist her up on it, and fuck her brains out, she'd be in.

And I, a lowly male, was supposed to keep it casual and hold to the idiotic vow I'd made only an hour before not to sleep with her?

Yeah, talk about a fucking idiot.

Sex would surely complicate things, and we had both just agreed to simple. Easy. Casual.

I leaned in and cupped her face. What could be more casual than a kiss? We'd stop after just one . . .

Chapter Thirteen

Smith

Lightning. That's what it felt like, kissing Evie.

The shock of adrenaline coursed through my veins, every cell coming to life at once. Her lips were so soft, I fought the urge to clamp my teeth on that bottom one, hard.

She, on the other hand, wasn't holding back. One second, we were both seated at the table, and the next, she'd slid from her chair half onto mine as she pressed herself tightly against me.

My hands made their way up to tangle in her silky hair, and she whimpered. The sound traveled straight to my cock, making it swell even more. I wondered briefly if the science of having literally all the blood in my body draining to my cock would kill me, but then she hitched one leg over my chair to straddle me, and I no longer gave a shit.

If I dropped dead right now, it would be with a smile on my lips.

I forced myself to release her hair, but only so I could free up my hands and push us back from the table. The maneuver opened up a whole new world of real estate, and I cupped Evie's round ass in both hands. She gasped into my mouth, which only encouraged me to tighten my grip.

She pulled back a few inches. "Smith," she murmured, running the tip of her finger over my mouth before crushing her lips to mine again.

Every muscle in my body was tense, primed, and ready to stand with her in my arms and carry her to my bedroom, but I still had one working brain cell, and it was bleating outraged commands.

Retreat!

Don't go even one step further.

You made a vow.

But that vow seemed so far away, blurred by the havoc Evie Reed was wreaking in my lap. I sucked in a breath through my nose, trying to work up the discipline to pull back, when she swept her tongue along mine and simultaneously ground her pussy against my cock.

I gripped her ass tighter, working her over my shaft again until she started moving on her own, writhing against me, making desperate little whimpering sounds that tugged at the last of my self-control.

The friction we were creating sucked the air from me, and for a second, all I could hear was the pounding of my heartbeat.

"Smith. Please," she murmured into my mouth, the break in her voice filling me with hot lust.

Vows were meant to be broken. Besides, no one could be expected to turn down an offer like this one. The woman I'd been fantasizing about for two weeks was rubbing all up on me, hot, wet, and ready for my cock.

And she's your best friend's sister.

The thought of Cullen—the lies I'd already told him, the lies I would continue to tell—had me freezing in place. It took Evie a second to realize I was no longer kissing her back and my questing hands had stilled, but when she did, she groaned.

"Nooo," she muttered as she pulled away. "Smith, don't think about him. I'm not a child anymore. I'm a grown woman, and I get to live my own life and make my own choices." As if to prove it, she leaned in and plastered her magnificent tits against my chest.

I met her gaze and bit back my own groan of frustration. Her face was flushed with unquenched need, her hair mussed from my fingers, her lips plump and damp. I'd never wanted to fuck like I did right now. My blood sang with it. Every instinct was urging me to finish the job I'd started. To drive inside that sweet little cunt until she screamed my name and I exploded inside her.

But until I knew what this was between us? Until I knew I could offer Evie more than I'd ever managed to give a woman before? Until then, I had to resist, because sharing a dinner and a kiss with your best friend's sister was bad. But knowingly taking her to bed without having any idea of what was going to happen after that? That was unforgivable.

In fact, if I were in Cullen's shoes and Evie was Pam? I'd have cut Cullen's balls off for even thinking about it.

My cock pulsed once and wept a single tear as I patted her ass lightly and slid her from my lap to stand.

"I'd love for you to stay a while longer. Have dessert. Watch a movie. But we can't sleep together, Evie. Not now. Not yet. Once we cross that line, there's no going back, and I need to make sure I'm worthy of the gift you want to give me." *And that the fallout will be something we can both live with.*

I kept that last part to myself, though, because I didn't want her blaming Cullen's overprotectiveness for me backing away. The fact was, there was a part of me that needed time outside her circle of hotness to think straight. Not any part below the waist, of course, but somewhere in my cranium, I knew that Cullen was only part of the problem. My fucked-up childhood—moving from foster home to foster home before being adopted— had left a space inside me where trust used to live. Too many times, I'd let myself be lulled by a warm hug and a soft heart. I let hope in, and then just when I thought things would be all right, I'd been ripped away again. New family. New problems.

After a while, it had become more than clear that hope was the enemy. *Expect the least, and you'll never be disappointed.* The Smith Hamilton human-relationships credo.

So it had been easy enough to keep a distance between myself and the women I slept with. If they opted out after a few weeks, it was fine because I'd never really opted in.

With Evie, that wasn't an option.

I was either in or out, because I cared. A lot. A lot more than I ever expected to. And the last thing I wanted to do was hurt her.

"You're a great guy, Smith. I'm not asking for a proposal, you know. I just want you to be my first real lover, is all," she said softly.

The word "first" implied there would be more after me, and the thought sent a hot knife of jealousy straight through me. It was all I could do not to say *fuck it* and take her right there. Make her forget that any other man even existed.

That inclination alone was enough to sober me and get my mind right.

"I want to hang out with you, Evie. I want us to spend more time together, but until we've got some idea of what exactly this is, we have to keep it in the friend zone. Can we do that?" I asked, watching her face for clues as to whether I was asking for too much.

She nodded slowly and ran a trembling hand through her hair. "I think I'd like that. I—I had fun too. I definitely want to spend more time together. And no telling Cullen anything, agreed?"

"Agreed."

She excused herself to the bathroom, and I was grateful for the reprieve as I cleaned up the dishes. It was going to be tough, but there was a sense of relief there too. At least I'd get to spend more time with Evie, and for now, that was enough.

• • •

Three hours later, though, as I watched her drive away, it was far from enough.

I was a man on a ledge again.

After watching a rom-com—her choice, and a drama—mine, we'd wound up snuggled together on the couch. It was long past midnight, and I'd wanted nothing more than to carry her into my bedroom and kiss her until that sleepy look disappeared. She'd been the strong one then, getting up and giving me a light peck on the mouth before gathering up her things.

"This was really nice, Smith. Thank you." The regret on her face was almost completely concealed as I walked her to her car and she slid in.

"Text me when you get home," I said, patting the hood of the car.

I made it all the way back into my living room before I had my pants unzipped and my cock in hand.

"Fu-uck," I groaned, the ache in my groin making the pressure of my hand almost painful.

I dropped back onto the couch, my face just an inch from where Evie's head had been, and breathed in the scent of her shampoo. Squeezing my eyes closed, I stroked my shaft up and down. Long, easy strokes for as long as I could stand it, and then faster. I let all the mental footage I had of Evie form a movie, filling in the gaps in my perverted imagination. What I came up with was the best porno in the world, and my heart knocked against my ribs so hard, I could hear it as I worked my cock over.

"I want you to come inside me, Smith," she whispered as she rode me up and down, faster and faster.

She pressed two fingers to her clit and moved them in a gentle circular motion as she impaled herself all the way onto my distended cock, taking me in to the hilt. Her pussy clenched, gently at first, but then harder as her nipples went tight and she threw her head back.

"Yes, yes!"

"Yes" was fucking right, because I was right behind her. My muscles tensed and my cock went rock hard. A second later, I bellowed her name and white light shot behind my eyelids as I came on my stomach in spurts.

My breath was still sawing in and out of my lungs when my cell phone buzzed and Evie's text lit up my screen.

EVIE: Made it.

Christ, that made two of us.

My low laugh was more of a groan as I snagged a

handful of tissues from the coffee table.

After I cleaned off, I thumbed out a quick reply.

SMITH: See you soon.

I realized with a start that, even if it was tomorrow, it wouldn't be soon enough. I didn't know I was starving until I'd tasted her.

Chapter Fourteen

Evie

"What's going on with you today?" Cullen chuckled, giving me a confused look.

The smile on my lips faded. "Nothing."

It was a total lie. I was still on a total high from my might-have-been-a-date with Smith last weekend. Maggie had said it wasn't a date—it was just two friends who had almost banged while hanging out—but I disagreed. The chemistry that buzzed between us was impossible to ignore.

And so even though I was sitting at work bright and early on a Monday morning, I was humming, my feet kicked up on my desk.

Cullen shook his head. "It's nice to see you feeling so cheery."

Smith shot me a smile. "Did you get laid last weekend or something?"

I almost swallowed my tongue.

"Don't you dare fucking answer that," Cullen said, looking distraught while I erupted in laughter.

Smith's playful side wasn't one that came out often, but I loved the rare glimpses he gave me into who he really was and how his mind worked.

It was the part afterward that made me twitchy.

"Speaking of getting laid, Smith, what's up with the new lady?" Cullen asked.

My heart jumped up into my throat.

Smith played it cool. "Nothing really."

"Don't play coy. You said it was someone from your past . . . so, who is she?"

Smith's gaze flashed to mine with something that looked like concern. "It's casual," he said, directing his attention back to my brother.

"Isn't it always with you, my man?" Cullen said with a wide grin.

A minute later, I managed to remove myself from the conversation with a mumbled excuse about needing to get something done, but for the rest of the morning, the scene replayed in my head.

This thing was supposed to be exactly that. Casual. What did it matter if Smith was seeing other women?

But, God, did it matter. I couldn't get it out of my mind. If I kept this up with Smith—seeing him, flirting with him, *kissing* him—was I setting myself up for the heartbreak of the century?

Taking another sip of coffee from my trusty to-go mug, I opened up the design program to review the campaign I'd finished last week.

As I looked at the images of boy shorts and camisoles in the new spring line, in spite of my heartache over the reminder of Smith's bad-boy nature, my mind wandered to much racier things . . .

The way Smith's full, sensual mouth slid over terms like *lace bodice*, *sweetheart cut*, and *ruching* made my panties wet. And instead of teasing me for my overly complicated drink order like Cullen would have, Smith memorized the damn thing. A triple-shot venti soy-mocha latte with no whip. And delivered it to my desk without fanfare. No big production. No thank-you required. He gave it to me because he wanted to, knowing it would make me happy. Simple as that. Just the fact that a man was willing to do that for me without getting anything in return sparked something inside me.

The hardest part of all of this was that after our brief encounter, it wasn't the sex that stuck with me. It was the intimacy that I missed. The way he'd gathered me up in his arms, pulled me in close to his chest—close enough to feel his body heat, to hear the steady thump of his heartbeat.

I missed the care he took with me, the tenderness I felt when his fingers moved over my skin, tucked a stray lock of hair behind my ear. I hadn't felt that kind of close connection with a man in a long time.

This might have been about sex when I started, but it had grown into something more. I didn't want just sex like I'd initially thought. No, I wanted a man. And the man I wanted was Smith.

The building's shared receptionist/secretary, Marjorie, poked her head into our office, and I resisted the urge to fan my face.

"You feeling okay, Evie? You look a little flushed," she said, cocking her head as her perceptive blue eyes tried to peer into my soul.

She was a perfect secretary. Shared by all the tenants who rented offices in this building, she was the glue that held everything together. Super organized and a real scheduling wiz, but times like this, I wish she were just a tiny bit less observant.

I cleared my throat and pressed a hand to my cheek. "Yeah, I, uh . . . stopped at the gym during lunch for a yoga class. It's been a while, so I'm a little overheated."

She stepped into my office and slid a file folder onto my desk. "Oh, cool, what gym?"

What gym, indeed—liar, liar, pants on fire?

"It's not really a *gym* gym, per se. It's like, you know how they have pop-up restaurants around the city? There are pop-up yoga classes. It's sort of an underground thing, so that's probably why you haven't heard of it."

Or maybe it was the fact that they only existed in my all-too-fertile imagination?

"Ooh, that sounds so cool! When is the next one? I'll go with you."

I let out a semi-hysterical laugh that I disguised as a cough. "See, that's the thing. You never know. Every so often, they just . . . pop up."

Her brow furrowed and she opened her mouth like she was going to ask more questions, but then seemed to think better of it. "Interesting. Well, in any case, keep it up. You're positively glowing."

She hurried out of the office, and the second she closed the door behind her, I folded in half and banged my forehead on my desk with a groan.

Smith wasn't even in the room, and he was still wreaking havoc on me. My brother noticed me acting weird, and even the receptionist had known something was up. If Smith and I didn't have sex—and *soon*—I was pretty sure I was going to wind up in a room with padded walls.

I snatched up the file folder and managed to get lost in work for a while. Once I had come up with a new design concept for an ad, I headed into the copy room so

I could blow up the printed version to tack on my wall and see it side by side with the last one to make sure they were different enough, but still cohesive.

I had just tugged the still-warm sheet of paper from the copier when goose bumps popped up on my arms. A second later, warm hands slid around my midriff.

"Want to play bad boss and naughty secretary with me?"

Smith's breath tickled my ear, and my nipples instantly went hard.

"Smith, let me go. What if—"

"Marjorie and your brother are on a conference call in the conference room down the hall. They'll be at least ten minutes," he murmured, nipping at my earlobe in a way that shot a bolt of heat straight through my body.

Or they could get done early, and one of them could walk in.

But I couldn't get the words out because Smith's hands were sliding up from my waist, higher until he closed them over my breasts. I gasped, and the sheet of paper fell from my limp fingers and fluttered to the floor.

He pressed forward until I was pinned against the machine and could feel every inch of his rock-hard length against my ass.

Instinctively, I ground my bottom against him, tearing a groan from his throat. My heart fluttered madly as he toyed with my nipples, rocking his hips against me.

We shouldn't be doing this. It was a risk that could yield horrific consequences. But, God, he felt good.

"Your body haunts me," he muttered, his voice hoarse in my ear. "Every time I close my eyes, I think of how sweet that pussy is."

I swallowed hard and reached behind me, wedging my hand between us to grab hold of his cock. "I think about you too."

Was that voice even mine? It was so raw, so low and full of need. I squeezed his shaft hard, and he bucked against my hand.

One second, I was pinned against the machine, and the next, he was wheeling me around to face him. His hazel eyes blazed gold as he looked down at me.

"I hadn't even meant to come in here. I was going to the men's room to wash my hands, but I smelled that scent and had to follow it. Then, there you were. That sexy silhouette. That ass. Those legs. You're like a fucking magnet."

I managed a grin as I ground against him. "And you're like steel."

He let out a growl and dived at my mouth, slanting his lips over mine. Ten minutes, he'd said. I couldn't help but wonder if both of us couldn't come in three. I knew I could. I was already on the edge.

My entire body tingled as he swept his tongue over mine, fucking me through my clothes with hard, rolling thrusts. I curled my arms around his waist and cupped his ass, plastering him tighter against me. His kisses grew rougher, all finesse gone now, and I loved it. This Smith—wild Smith . . . risk-taker Smith—was the Smith I'd always admired. And I couldn't deny he was bringing out that side of me too. A side that I'd let go untapped for far too long.

I bounced my hips against him, wishing we were skin to skin, arching helplessly now as my body attempted to relieve the ache. It was only getting worse, spreading lower, stretching like taffy in the sun. I had no idea what had caused this change in him since at dinner he'd seemed intent on playing the perfect gentleman, but I liked this reckless side to him.

I pulled my head back but didn't stop arching against him. "What if we lock the door?" I whispered, now desperate for it. That satisfaction only Smith could give me.

He groaned and pressed his forehead against mine. "Jesus, Evie, I want to. You have no idea how much I want to. But if the two of us are in here with the door locked, that's a dead giveaway. Especially if you walk out looking like this."

His cock was hitting me in exactly the right spot, and I had to choke back a whimper. "Look like what? I look the same as I always do."

His laugh sounded pained. "No. Your lips are pink and swollen. Your nipples are hard and your eyes are drunk with desire. In a word? You look like you've been fucking."

If only.

But suddenly, a noise echoed down the hallway.

"So then we'll call him back right before end of business," Cullen said, presumably to Marjorie.

"Break time is over." Smith stepped back with a sad half smile on his lips as he straightened my blouse. "I'm going to have to borrow your file folder, though."

My pulse pounded hard as I nodded, still in a daze. "Sure."

I didn't know what he meant to do with it until he held it in front of his cock like a shield. Laughter threatened to bubble from me, and I slapped my hand over my mouth.

He held a finger up to his lips. "Shh." He dropped one last kiss to the tip of my nose and backed toward the door. "I'll drop this off to you later," he said, gesturing to the file folder. Then he disappeared out the door.

I could hear him talking with Cullen down the hall, so I waited for a full five minutes before leaving the little copy room. Not just because I didn't want to run into

Cullen, but because that was how long it took to get my legs back under me and steady.

Smith Hamilton was packing some seriously powerful stuff. So powerful, in fact, that I had to wonder how any woman resisted him.

The feel of his hands tangled in my hair, the swell of his cock between my legs. In those few stolen moments, so much had changed.

He wanted me. Maybe just as badly as I wanted him.

And now that I knew that? All bets were off. I was willing to fight for my man.

Chapter Fifteen

Smith

Damn . . . that kiss, though.

My brain instantly supplied a mental replay, and I shifted my dick in my pants to make sitting behind a desk bearable.

Jesus, sometimes I wondered if I had a screw loose or something, because I couldn't make this whole thing any harder on myself if I tried. Not to mention that my thoughtless move could have jeopardized everything good in my life—my job, my relationship with Evie, my friendship with her brother.

What if Cullen had walked in?

All of his possible reactions flitted through my mind, and I winced. At the very least, some blood would have been shed, whether it was mine, his, or both.

But for some reason, I couldn't have stopped myself if I'd tried. Once I saw Evie there, bent over the copy machine, her bottom lip pinched between those white teeth, I was done. It was like I was on autopilot. My body moved toward hers as if controlled by some otherworldly gravitational pull.

I gritted my teeth and drummed my fingers on the desk in front of me in frustration.

This was torture. Spending time with someone I liked as much as I liked Evie, wanting her more than I'd ever wanted anything in my life and not being able to have her, it made me feel like an addict. Twitchy, needy, and sort of desperate.

Not a feeling I was accustomed to at all. And not a feeling I liked one bit.

What it we gave in? Tonight, even. What if I texted her right now and asked her to meet me at my apartment after work and put an end to our shared misery?

Then what about tomorrow when we go back to being friends?

I swallowed a bitter laugh and raked a hand over my face.

"Here are the numbers you asked for," a male voice murmured.

Adam, my assistant and an all-around nice guy, waited near my desk with a file folder in hand. I'd been so distracted, I hadn't even heard him come in.

"Thanks, I appreciate it." I took the folder without further comment, and then looked up a minute later when I realized that he was still hovering.

He cleared his throat and shifted from foot to foot. "I know it's none of my business, but are you okay? You've been looking sort of weird lately. Not sick, but . . . stressed. Distracted, maybe." He perched his glasses higher on his nose and shrugged. "You don't have to tell me if you don't want to, but I wanted to make sure you're not working too hard or if there is something more I should be doing on my end to clear your plate."

I closed the file folder and blew out a sigh. I'd been dividing my time between the two offices—this one that my family ran like a well-oiled machine whether I was here or not, and of course, the new office for Sophia's headquarters.

"Yeah, sorry about that. I hope I'm not being too much of an asshole." I weighed my options and decided on a half truth. "It's been difficult juggling my work here with the consulting work I'm doing at Sophia's."

Adam crinkled his nose. "You sure that's all it is? It's not like you to let work bog you down."

"Okay, the truth is work is going well, so no worries there. I've got a woman on the brain. I like her and she likes me, but there's a raft of shit in the way. I gotta admit, the whole thing is getting to me a little."

A relieved smile tugged at his lips, and I realized then that my poker face wasn't as good as I'd thought. Poor Adam had been worried that I was going to fire him or something. Totally my fault, because I probably walked around this place looking like I was about to claw the bark off trees and start roaring.

Not cool.

Plus, with my new gig, I'd been spending very little time in this office lately.

"I hear you there, boss. I've got a girlfriend too, and she's bugging me about not having an engagement ring yet and all that. It can really get to a guy," Adam said, looking a little shaken at the mention of an engagement ring. "If you ever want to meet for a beer after work and blow off some steam, let me know. I'm always down."

I nodded and grinned at him. "I might take you up on that. Thanks."

Adam backed out of my office and closed the door behind him, leaving me alone with my thoughts again. Sure as shit, I almost begged him to come back, because my thoughts were confounding as fuck.

There had to be a logical explanation for this. Working alongside Evie day by day had clouded my brain. Her citrusy scent that was burned into my nostrils, the sound of her laugh when she really let go, her passion for her work—all of it had left an impression that I couldn't shake.

Shit, I even liked watching the way she contributed at work. She enjoyed pretty things, and took pride in her work making our web presence more visually appealing. I liked that when she needed inspiration, she'd flip through fabric swatches, finger squares of delicate lace, toy with pieces of buttery-soft satin, line up neat rows of tiny pearl buttons until her next wave of brilliance struck. She was young but she was savvy, and it was incredible to watch her use her God-given talents to create something good in the world.

All in all, my work with Sophia's was certainly far more interesting than the number-crunching I did all day long for my parents' company.

My cell rang, and I snatched it up without even glancing at the number, happy for another distraction.

"This is Hamilton," I murmured, thumbing through the file Adam had brought.

"Smith? It's Arabella Christianson from Château Prive."

I stiffened and glanced at my desk calendar. *Fuck*. A knot formed in the pit of my stomach. Arabella's boutiques were one of Sophia's newest, most high-profile retailers. I had a call scheduled with her tomorrow to discuss upping our shipments. Not to mention, she and I had a sordid history.

Just be cool.

"Hello, Arabella, good to hear from you. I hope I didn't mix my days up?" I was pretty sure that wasn't the case. Adam kept a tight rein on my schedule, but I couldn't think of any possible good news that would have her calling me a day early, and I definitely wasn't in the market for any bad news.

"No, we're still on for tomorrow, but I wasn't sure whether to call you or Cullen," she said, her tone chilly. "I'm having an issue with your social media director."

Evie.

Shit.

I cleared my throat and sat up a little straighter, my brain already churning out potential ways to put out whatever fire was smoldering. The good news was Arabella had called me first and not Cullen. The bad news was I didn't know if I was going to be able to help Evie, and this might have to escalate anyway.

"What's going on?"

"Well, she was supposed to send me a mock-up for the social media advertising campaign yesterday, and I still haven't received it. My concern is that if you people can't meet a simple deadline for some shared advertising, how can I expect you to meet our shipment deadlines once we increase?"

Her voice grew more clipped by the second, and I could tell she was building up a serious head of steam.

"When Cullen told us he was expanding and could push out product more quickly, we took him at his word. I have seventeen stores prepping premium front-of-the-store space for the new line as we speak. If those spaces are empty come delivery time—"

"They won't be," I said simply, cutting in before she could lob a threat that would really piss me off.

Our personal shit was set aside. I was here to help Cullen make his company a financial success again, not to let myself get all pissed off and defensive on behalf of Evie. But, damn it, Evie was good at her job. No way she'd just blown off this deadline. I'd seen her bustling around the office all last week, muttering to herself about this very campaign. Something smelled fishy, and I was going to get to the bottom of it.

"Arabella, I'm not sure exactly what happened, but I'm going to find out. Evie is the most responsible person I know, so I do believe there is an explanation. Give me fifteen minutes to get it and call you back, all right?"

For a second, I thought she might have hung up, but then she let out an exasperated huff.

"Fine. Fifteen minutes," she snapped before breaking the connection.

Just fucking dandy. I stuffed my phone in my pocket and made a beeline to the elevator. Thankfully, Sophia's office was only a seven-minute walk from here.

When I reached the office, Evie was standing with her back to the door, facing a back wall that was covered with images of women in gorgeous lingerie. The splashes of color and the layout of her presentation were so eye-catching, I found myself distracted for an instant by the sheer punch of it.

"Hey, Smith, everything okay?"

She blushed a little as our gazes connected, and for a moment, I was silent as the memory of our kiss passed between us again.

"Uh, yeah. Wait. No." I scrubbed a hand over my jaw and motioned for the two of us to sit. "Look, I just got a call from Arabella Christianson. She said you were supposed to send her your proposed ad campaign yesterday."

Evie's brows drew into a frown as her cheeks drained of color. "No. That's not correct. I have it here in my notes . . ." She turned and began riffling through a pile of papers on her desk, tugging one out and holding it aloft. "This is due by end of business today. I still have a few hours."

She slid the page across the desk to me. Sure enough, the time and date were written there in Evie's graceful script and underlined twice.

That was good, but it would only take me so far. In her mind, Arabella still believed the agreement was for yesterday.

"I figured as much. You're never late on anything, and I know how hard you've been working on this. Did you firm up these plans via e-mail or phone?"

"Shit. I'm pretty sure it was on the phone." Evie shot a glance over her shoulder and turned back to me, looking as vulnerable as I'd ever seen her. "This would suck if it reflects on us poorly because, to be honest, it's been done for two days. I've just been putting off sending it until the last minute because I'm nervous that she won't like it."

"That's not possible. I know Arabella."

"Arabella?" Evie paused, her eyes narrowing. "What's the story? Is there something I should know?"

I cleared my throat. "It was a long time ago." And not something I wanted to get into with Evie—ever.

"And what, you're older and wiser now?" Her eyes narrowed further into the shape of slivered almonds, and I felt my stomach tense.

"Yes, and more importantly, I know how to show some restraint."

"What does that mean exactly, Smith?"

"It means you have nothing to worry about." That part was true.

"Why would I be worried? There's nothing between us, right?"

"The truth is, she and I have a history. Let me go smooth this over. I'm afraid she's got some old hang-ups, and this really isn't about you at all."

Evie shot me a now wide-eyed glare, curiosity written all over her features.

"She and I were connected in the past. And she might be trying to sabotage you to punish me. I'll handle it."

"No way. You're not fighting my battle. And what kind of relationship?"

"It was purely physical." The words felt sour in my throat. I hated admitting this to Evie, but I wouldn't lie to her.

"So you slept with her?"

"Like I said, it was a long time ago."

The moment the words left my mouth, I hated myself. The look of disappointment that flashed on Evie's features was brief but unmistakable. A few seconds of silence passed between us, and I was left feeling like even more of an asshole than I was.

I shook my head slowly and took another long look at the collage of campaign elements. "If Arabella doesn't like the campaign you created, then she's a fucking idiot,

Evie. This is brilliant."

And it was. She'd struck the perfect balance between sensuality and class, each image showcasing the pieces to their best advantage. One teddy in particular caught my eye and I cocked my head, imagining Evie in that very outfit.

"That color would look amazing on your skin," I murmured softly, my voice dropping to a whisper. "You'd look am—"

"Fucking horrible in that outfit," a low voice chimed in sharply from behind me. "Ew, Smith. Don't be imagining my little sister in this shit, or I'm going to have to fire you both," Cullen said, stepping between us.

Evie's cheeks turned the color of cooked beets, but I managed to keep it together.

"It's a pretty color, buddy," I said with a grin. "It would look great with her hair. Don't get your panties in a wad."

Cullen grunted and then shrugged. "Whatever. Still gross. The three of us need to have a quick discussion about the new line with manufacturing in an hour, so clear your schedules, all right?"

Evie gave her brother a thumbs-up, and I nodded. "Sure thing."

He turned on his heel and left, already on to the next thing, seeming to forget all about the fact that I'd been imagining his sister in a peach teddy. That didn't help either Evie or me, though, because we were left gazing at each other guiltily.

"I'm going to go see if I can talk Arabella down," I said, breaking the tension. "And if not, don't stress. I know that once she sees this, all will be forgotten anyway."

Evie gave me a grateful smile and waved. I'd made it all the way to the door before I couldn't stop myself from turning back.

"You would look super hot in that lingerie, though. Just saying."

A pair of satin panties whizzed past my face, hitting the door frame. When I looked back at Evie, she was casting a scowl in my direction.

●●●

Once at home, I felt the stirrings of a headache forming. Huffing out a deep breath, I sat down on the side of my bed. I just needed a fucking minute here. I raked a hand through my hair, feeling the weight of all this new pressure on my shoulders.

Reaching into the drawer of my nightstand, I pulled a worn slip of paper from inside a familiar envelope. The paper's edges were soft, and the faded ink reflected its age. As much as it evoked memories of my less-than-desirable beginnings, it was almost comforting in a way too.

I was left at four years old with just the clothes on my back—a size too small and fraying at the edges—along with this note in the parking lot of an emergency room downtown. My fingers traced the barely legible scrawl absently. I remembered nothing of my life before, and my adoptive mom said that was a good thing, but I wasn't so sure. Even some sad memories would have helped me piece together the fragments of my early childhood.

The blank space was left to fester, growing wider, deeper with each passing year. It was an emptiness inside me that nothing in my life had been able to fill—and believe me, I'd tried. Booze. Women. Fast cars. I'd tried it all.

Now I'd resigned myself to live with that hole in my chest. I kept my head down, throwing myself into my work to compensate for the missing puzzle piece inside me. But what else could I do?

I stuffed the paper back inside its resting place, knowing I was about to get deeper into my own issues before I found my way back out again.

Chapter Sixteen

Evie

I was a walking cliché. The once-ugly duckling who had shed her baby fat and awkward phase but was still too chickenshit to believe she was pretty.

I let out a heavy sigh, checking my appearance one more time. I might not like what I saw in my reflection, but that was silly, right? Smith saw me that way. He saw me as a sexual woman who'd wanted to explore, someone smart and capable and funny. He even said I'd look beautiful in that lacy peach lingerie. We worked in the business of seductive undergarments, but I'd never let myself believe I would be wearing them for a man, let alone Smith, of all people.

Fuck it.

Turning on my heel, I grabbed my purse and strutted from my apartment.

I wouldn't know unless I tried . . .

Chapter Seventeen

Smith

Meet me at Restaurant Saint Germaine at seven on Friday.

I glanced at my text to Evie once more just to confirm the time and then checked my watch. Five after. She was always punctual, if not early, and I was starting to think I was about to get the blow-off.

The week at work had gone by at a snail's pace. Once I'd smoothed over the whole cock-up with Arabella, largely helped by the fact that Evie had indeed hit the ad campaign out of the park, there had only been mundane number-crunching to focus on. That left way too much brain space for me to think about Evie. The kiss in the copy room, and most of all, our date tonight.

I settled into my seat at a corner booth of the famed restaurant and glanced at the door again.

If there was even going to be a date.

She'd said yes when I texted her the other day, but maybe the weirdness of witnessing Cullen's response to our exchange had finally gotten to her and she'd chickened out. I wouldn't blame her one bit. It was fucking weird for me too. But things had escalated to the point that I was past caring. We would deal with Cullen when the time came.

For now, I knew that I was on the cusp of something with Evie. Something special. Something I'd never felt before. Something that was equal parts intriguing and maddening. Something that had the potential to quiet the demons inside me that whispered in the dark of night that I was unlovable and bound to be alone for life.

It might even be—

"Hey, you!"

I looked up to see Evie standing next to the table wearing a cream-colored blouse and a black leather skirt that fit like a second skin. Her hair was up in an elaborate twist that made me want to yank out the pins just to see those curls go tumbling around her shoulders.

My heart stuttered in my chest, and I stood. "You look amazing," I murmured softly, leaning in to kiss her cheek. I breathed in her scent while I was at it, and my cock stood at immediate attention.

"Thank you," she replied, her smile a little shy. "The skirt is a little much for me . . . kind of racy, but I figured what the hell?"

What the hell, indeed? I resisted the urge to skim my fingers across the buttery-soft leather and cup a handful of ass, and instead gestured for her to sit.

"I wish you'd let me pick you up next time," I said, sitting back down across from her.

"After the close calls we've had with Cullen lately?" she said with a snort. "Our luck, he'd be pulling in for a surprise visit right as we walked out. Uber is fine. If you want to take me home tonight, though . . ."

She trailed off, her eyes blazing, and my pulse raced to warp speed.

"Ma'am, may I off-air you a beverahge?" the waiter who had magically appeared asked in the thickest, most put-on French accent I'd ever heard.

Evie blinked up at him, her brow furrowed. "I'm sorry, what did you say?"

He smiled, but there was an edge of annoyance as he replied. "I said, what may I get you to drink?" His accent was no less obnoxious, but this time, she understood him because he added a pantomime of a person drinking from a glass, his pinkie extended.

"Uh, sure. I'll have . . ." She shot me a glance and I shrugged, motioning to my Scotch. I'd been spared this fake-accent routine because I'd ordered mine at the bar before sitting, so she was on her own. "A glass of chardonnay, please."

He bent in half in a deep bow, nearly beaning his head on the corner of the table, and Evie winced.

"I weel return momentarily weez your libation," he said before turning on his heel and sauntering away.

Evie stared after him and then turned to me. "Holy crap," she murmured, and burst out laughing.

I'd always loved that laugh. It rocked her whole body and rang through the room. Apparently, though, not everyone was as impressed. A pair of diners a few seats away sent disapproving glances our way. I kept the grin on my face and raised my glass to them before taking a deep swallow.

Fuck them. If Evie's contagious laugh didn't charm the pants off them, they were clearly raised by wolves.

When she finally stopped giggling, Evie held a hand to her heaving chest and shook her head. "I've been to some nice places in my life, but this one takes the cake. There are five forks, Smith. *Five.* Even I don't know what to do with that many," she whispered, jabbing a finger toward the gleaming utensils. "I'm feeling a little out of my element."

I was about to argue with her, to tell her she would fit in no matter where she went. But the truth was, when I'd planned the date, I just wanted to impress her. This place was a Michelin three-star restaurant and made all the magazines. After our first date at my apartment where we'd eaten a humble roasted chicken, I'd wanted to knock her socks off.

But that wasn't Evie, was it?

This was a generic fancy date for a generic woman. Evie was right. The only reason she was out of her element was because this place wasn't good enough for her.

I dug into my pocket, pulled out my wallet, and dropped a fifty on the table. Then I stood and held out my hand. "Come on. Let's get the fuck out of here."

She let out a puzzled laugh and eyed me suspiciously. "And go where?"

"You'll see," I replied, a plan already unfolding in my mind.

Tonight would be a night Evie would never forget, and it wouldn't be because of any stars or fancy food. It would be because the date was for us and only us.

• • •

"I thought this place closed down last year," she said, shooting me a shocked look as we pulled up to Rap Scallion's Bar and Grill less than an hour later.

"Nope. Granted, nobody we know comes here anymore because it's still a college bar, but they're open and it's Friday Five-Cent Wing night, and they have a trivia contest going on."

When her eyes went suspiciously glassy, I knew I'd done good. This was the same bar we'd gone to on her twenty-first birthday. Up until the point that she'd lost her cookies, she'd had a great night. We all did. Sometimes I wondered if I'd known then that things had changed between us and had refused to admit it to myself.

"Thank you for bringing me here. Lots of great memories," she said, reaching out a hand and laying it gently on my chest. She shifted on the seat of my car and then gasped. "Oh my God, but look at what I'm wearing. I think I'm just a little overdressed, no?"

"Except that one time you were naked in my hotel-room bed, you always seem overdressed to me, so I'm not the guy to ask," I said with a wink. "But I can help if you're worried about it." I shrugged off my suit jacket and tossed my tie aside before facing her again. "Let's get this hair down first."

I reached for the twist like I'd been dying to do since she first walked into the restaurant, and with a few gentle tugs, sent the whole mass tumbling down in a cascade of honey waves. I ran my fingers through it until it looked sexy and mussed, like she'd just left my bed.

"Perfect," I murmured, my voice gritty.

Her throat worked as she swallowed and nodded. "Good start. What else?"

I trailed my hands down her neck to the buttons of her blouse, flipping open one and then another until a sexy hint of cleavage showed. It took a Herculean effort not to bury my face between her breasts and stay there until morning. I worked up one more surge of self-discipline and untucked the hem of her blouse, unfastening two buttons at the bottom as well and knotting it at her waist. It was only then that, in the moonlight, I realized I'd uncovered a swath of fabric.

Peach lace.

"Ahhh, fuck," I groaned. My gaze locked with hers, and her breathing became choppy as she wet her lips.

"Y-you said you wanted to see me in it," she whispered, her voice so low I had to lean in to hear her.

I sure had. In her office a few days before, I'd pointed to this very piece of lingerie. And now, here she was wearing it.

For me.

My resolve not to sleep with her was hanging by a fucking thread, and that thread was unraveling faster by the second.

"I want to see the rest of it more than you could possibly know." In fact, my dick was so hard, it could have crushed coal into diamonds. "But if I unfasten one more button, we're never getting out of this car."

"Would that be so bad?" she asked.

She gnawed on that bottom lip the way she always did, and I let my thumb caress just a scant inch of the soft fabric before pulling back.

"Yup. Because if you think your real first time is going to be in a car, you've lost your mind."

And if I didn't get out of said car, I was going to lose mine.

I pressed a hard, rough kiss to her mouth because I couldn't not do it, and then I flung open my door. "Now, let's go have some fun."

Luckily, we did. We strutted into Rap Scallion's hand

in hand like we owned the place. We got a few looks from the jeans-and-T-shirt crowd, but soon enough, everyone went back to their beers, and Evie and I were engaged in a heated battle at the dartboard.

"All I need is a bull's-eye and I win," she said, rubbing her hands together with glee as she lined up the tip of her high-heeled shoe with the piece of black tape that marked the floor. She closed one eye and perched the tip of her tongue on her top lip as she focused.

As competitive a person as I was, I felt a rush of pride wash over me as she launched that dart into the heart of the board. The electronic game beeped and blinked wildly in celebration of her victory, and she danced along with the noise in time.

"Oh yeah, oh yeah, I'm a beast!" she chanted, shimmying in place as I looked on, shaking my head in mock disappointment.

In truth, I could have watched her shimmy all night. A swath of that peach lace flashed at her waist whenever she moved, and it was doing things to my insides that I couldn't even describe.

I strolled toward her and bowed deeply like the waiter at the restaurant. "Congratulations, mademoiselle. May I buy you a victory drink?"

She grinned and nodded. "Yes, please. No Sex on the Beach, though. Shot and a beer for me."

We made our way back to the bar and I placed our drink order. While we waited, she sent me a grin that lit up the room.

"This was a great idea. I'm having a blast. Remember the night of my birthday, when we first got here we did that trivia contest? And Cullen made our team name Multiple Scorgasms?"

I laughed out loud at the memory. "That was awesome. And to be fair, we did crush it that night."

"We did. I think that was the last time I got to hang out with Pam. How is she doing?"

Thinking of my sister made me realize I hadn't shared the news yet. "Actually, she's pregnant again."

Evie stared at me before clapping a hand over her mouth. "For real? Holy shit, she's amazing. I don't know how she does it all. When I have kids, I think I'm going to need to . . . Never mind." She stopped short and blushed before taking a swallow of the beer the bartender had set in front of her.

"You're allowed to talk about the future and the things you want in life, Evie," I said gently.

Maybe our whole talk about being casual had made her afraid to talk to me about anything serious. That was a mistake. While I wanted to take things slow, it had become glaringly obvious in the past weeks that this was as serious as things had ever gotten for me.

"I didn't want you to think because I want kids one day that meant I expected them to be yours or whatever," she said, finally meeting my gaze.

The vulnerability in her eyes made me ache for her, and I leaned in and pressed my forehead against hers.

"I know that. And I'm not sure how this is all going to turn out, but I can tell you this. Thinking of you with someone else's babies makes me want to break shit. And if that's not casual, then too fucking bad."

Her grin was tremulous, and she traced a fingertip

over my mouth. "Yeah. Too fucking bad."

This was deep. Deeper than we'd gone so far, and part of me wanted to pull back.

Opening up about shit like this had always been a bone of contention between my ex and me. Talking about kids and the future had been terrifying. What if I was like my own father and found out that, once I had a kid, I didn't want to be a parent anymore? What if I was shitty at it, like my mother, and opted out when things got hard?

Time and time again, Karen had pressed. And time and time again, it had felt like an invasion of privacy. Eventually it became a no-fly zone, and we'd drifted apart with nothing real to sustain us.

But with Evie, even as I was about to change the subject and make a joke out of sheer habit, something stopped me. This didn't feel like an invasion at all. It felt right. Like getting something off my chest that had been sitting there like a weight for a very long time.

I cupped the back of her head and touched my lips gently to hers in the softest of kisses. For a long time, we stayed like that, breathing in sync, just holding each other, and damn if it didn't feel good.

I was falling, and I was falling hard. I could only hope Evie felt the same and that, soon enough, we'd come up with a way to tell her brother.

A way that wouldn't drive us all apart and ruin everything.

Chapter Eighteen

Evie

It was late and way past my bedtime, but I had no desire to end this and go home.

Smith and I had moved to a little booth beside the bar, and I was trying to keep it together, despite the fact that his jealousy had my heart singing. Why would a man care who a woman had a baby with if he was just in it for the sex? And more to the point, why the hell weren't we *having sex* if he was just in it for the sex?

These were the questions that plagued me as we sat talking and nursing our next round of drinks. I quickly realized that thoughts like those were a descent into madness. I would literally drive myself crazy if I kept trying to analyze every word he spoke. Instead, I focused on the man in front of me.

I loved everything about tonight. The reservation he'd made at that swanky restaurant—and then promptly broken before stealing me away for a much more laid-back evening, which somehow had made the date even more intimate. Sharing laughs, telling stories, we'd been able to open up and be ourselves.

As I gazed into Smith's eyes, I realized that something about him being older made him so much more desirable and charming than other men. A beer-swilling, hamburger-eating, football-and-video-game junkie he was not. Or maybe it was just that guys my age were so juvenile compared to Smith. He had friends and family who loved him, an impressive job that he dressed in a suit for every day, and that was before he came in to help rescue Sophia's.

Everything about him was special and attractive to me. Just the life he'd built for himself was enviable. Most days I felt like a hot mess, munching on dry cereal from a plastic bag on my way into work, reading those sex-tips articles at night—hoping for inspiration. Yeah, I was a work in progress.

But Smith knew exactly who he was. A businessman, an athlete who enjoyed regular five-mile runs through the park on the weekends, a friend who could be relied on.

Or at least he did until I marched into his hotel room that night and confused everything.

"So, how do you like working for the company? Did you ever imagine you'd be working in women's undergarments?" I asked.

He let out a short chuckle. "No. Never. I've always enjoyed lingerie, but usually it's because I'm the one taking it off."

Now I was the one letting out a giggle.

"I do really like working there, but I'm just a numbers guy," he continued. "You and your brother are the true visionaries."

"Just a numbers guy." I rolled my eyes at him. "I'm pretty sure you're a millionaire, so yeah."

Shit. I shouldn't have said that. The drinks we'd downed were going to my head.

But Smith just shrugged. "My family is. I got lucky."

"You won the lottery with them."

Smith's family was amazing, but I hoped I hadn't just put my foot in my mouth.

We got quiet for a second. But I'd already started

down this path, so it only made sense to keep going.

"Do you ever wonder about your biological parents? If you have any siblings out there?"

Smith sat up straighter. "Of course I do."

"Have you ever looked into it? Hired a private investigator, anything like that?"

He shook his head. "I've thought about it, but no. Couldn't do that to my mom."

Mary. The woman who fostered, then adopted Smith was now simply Mom. It was sweet that he was so thoughtful, putting her feelings first, but this was his life too. Surely he was entitled to some basic information about where he came from.

"Do you want to know the truth?" he asked, and I nodded. "It gets to me sometimes, not knowing, living life as one big question mark. Even the little things like when I go to get a physical and the doctor wants my family's medical history, or wondering how I got my hazel eyes."

It was crazy how much I could know about this man, and yet he constantly still surprised me.

Reaching over, I placed my hand on his. "I never thought about that part of it. Being in a family with people who don't look like you."

"Yeah. Maybe someday, maybe when my parents pass away, I'll look into it. But you know, regardless, I don't think I'd change a thing," he said with a shrug. "Even after all the hard times early on. It was tough getting shuffled around, especially because I was so young and didn't understand. I wanted to be loved so badly and couldn't figure out why no one wanted to love me back."

His tone was so matter of fact, like that of a man far removed from that pain, but my throat ached with tears at the thought of a four-year-old Smith being packed up and moved from house to house.

I wanted to go back in time, find his birth mother and father and slap them both upside the head for leaving him. Sure, maybe they'd done it because they couldn't provide a good life for him anymore, but in my emotional state at that moment, none of that mattered. All that mattered was that Smith had suffered, and I hated the thought of it.

"My parents are really wonderful," he continued,

oblivious to my internal struggle. "And my relationship with Pam and her family is probably one of the best things in my life. I wouldn't trade that for the world."

I nodded in agreement. Cullen and I were close like that, and it was a bond that could never be broken.

At least, I hope not.

I took a sip from my glass and tried not to let myself indulge in that line of thinking. If Cullen did find out about Smith and me and that was enough to damage our relationship for good, then there were deeper problems at play. We were family, and we would work through it if it came down to that. It was Cullen and Smith's relationship that had me worried. As close as they were, it was still hard for Cullen to accept that I was a grown-up now. He would probably think Smith had taken advantage of me, which, considering how we'd started whatever this was between us, was almost funny.

"But I do think my past fucked me up some and probably has a lot to do with my relationships as an adult. I won't lie, Everleigh," he said, meeting my gaze. "I feel different about you than I've ever felt before, but I don't know what that means yet. I'm no white knight, and I could fuck this all up. If you want to walk away now and cut your losses, I'll understand."

God, had it only been a couple of weeks ago that I'd climbed into his bed? So much had changed so quickly. How strange my only goal back then was to get a do-over. To have my first orgasm with a man, and have Smith be the guy at the other end of the dick I needed to get me there. How quickly that had changed.

Yeah, I still wanted that. More every day, actually. But now, as we sat talking about our hopes and dreams and families? I found myself wishing that this was my life. Smith and me talking about our day, laughing at darts and sharing our lives with each other.

That was dangerous shit, and I needed to watch my step. But I wasn't walking away. Not yet.

"And miss all the fun? Not a chance," I replied, trying to keep my tone light so he couldn't see how much this meant to me. He claimed to be no white knight, but the Smith I knew would back off instantly if he realized the power he had over me. If and when this ended, I would be destroyed. Only I couldn't let him know that.

In an effort to take a step back from the intimacy and catch my breath, I shot him a grin before plucking a five-dollar bill from my purse.

"Why don't we go play some music on the jukebox?"

I stood and waited for Smith to join me, and then headed over to the glowing monstrosity in the corner. Once it ate my money, we paged through, looking for songs we both liked.

"Oh my God, do you remember this one?" I jabbed my finger on "Remix to Ignition" by R. Kelly and closed my eyes for a second as the music started.

"How could I forget? You were like ten years old, and I walked in on you singing it into a brush that time. It was hilarious," Smith said, his eyes shining with laughter.

"By *hilarious*, you mean awesome, right? Because I'm pretty sure I was singing the shit out of this song."

I leaned in and belted out a few lines along with R. Kelly as Smith howled with laughter.

Yeah, this felt good. Too good to stop.

Major crash and burn ahead or not, I was committed

to staying on this ride with Smith and finding out when and where it ended. If I wound up with a broken heart, at least I had Maggie to comfort me, along with Ben and Jerry.

It would have to be enough.

Chapter Nineteen

Smith

Three weeks later

"And we just got a huge order from Saks." Cullen leaned forward, putting his arms on the table between us, and shook his head in amazement. "*Saks*. Smith, do you have any idea how long I've been waiting for an order from fucking Saks?"

I raised my eyebrows in approval as I bit into my massive roast beef sandwich, all the while trying not to follow Evie's movements with my gaze.

"Not to mention that the new line is on fire at every single retailer," Cullen continued, spooning up some of the chowder from his bowl and shooting me a wide grin.

We'd been at lunch for precisely four minutes before Evie had walked into the same little deli a few blocks from the office. She hadn't caught sight of us yet, but there was no doubt she would. I only hoped she'd have a little mercy on me and refuse our eventual invitation to join us.

She was wearing a new tailored pantsuit, and it hugged her bottom like a glove. It was hard enough trying to keep it together in the office day after day with her brother in the general area. When we were all forced to be in a room together, it was a living hell.

"From a sheer numbers perspective, we're outpacing even our most optimistic forecasts, so this is awesome," I said, digging into my potato salad as Evie passed our table.

In a stroke of perfect luck, she caught my eye right as Cullen's attention was focused on sprinkling oyster crackers into his soup. She must have been as uncomfortable with the thought of making it through a meal as part of this awkward threesome as I was, because she wiggled her fingers at me and tore ass out the door.

"I couldn't be happier," Cullen said, beaming. "Thanks so much for coming on to help out. Between you and Evie, it's been a game changer."

Me and Evie.

I chewed my food as I thought back on the past few days.

Had it really only been three weeks ago that we'd gone out to Rap Scallion's and played darts? It seemed like months. In the interim, we'd seen each other daily at work, and then again most evenings. Even if it was just the two of us meeting at a dive across town for a quick cocktail after her yoga class, or me surprising her by stopping at her place on the way to Pam's to steal a kiss.

Twice, she'd come over for movie night.

Twice, we'd missed half the movie, making out like teenagers on my couch.

And twice, she'd squirmed against my hand as she came for me.

My cock bucked in my pants as I recalled the heat of her. The scent of her. That tight fucking—

"Seriously, my little sis is on fire," Cullen said with a proud smile.

I nearly choked on my roast beef, forcing it down my dry throat with a long chug of water.

"What?" I said, my pulse jackhammering as I tried to clear the rest of the sandwich from my aching windpipe.

Cullen's brows drew together and he let out a laugh. "The social media stuff she's been putting together. The boutiques are all fighting over her now. They each want their own Evie campaign and are using her images as jump-off points for their window displays."

My heart rate slowed to something closer to normal, and I forced a tight smile. "Yeah, she's doing really well."

So well, in fact, that I had to credit a large part of the revenue hike to her efforts. I'd told Cullen that earlier in the week, but my own guilt made me wary of repeating it. Was I too complimentary? Was I too friendly toward her? Not friendly enough?

All in all, this was getting real fucking old. Something had to give, and soon. Besides the fact that I was in a near-constant state of arousal, I also had to wrestle with my conscience. I felt like a fraud. Here I was at lunch with Evie's brother, unable to stop thinking about my fingers working inside her, and that little break in her voice when she came.

Not cool. Not cool at all.

I managed to get through the rest of lunch without

choking, but the whole thing had left a bad taste in my mouth.

By the time we headed back to the office, I was feeling like shit on every level. For being a bad friend, for having to basically ignore Evie at the deli, and for not singing her praises as loudly as I should have been as far as work went because I didn't want Cullen giving me the side-eye.

I made a mental vow to take the coming weekend and make some major decisions about Evie and about my life. Somehow, I'd managed to keep my vow to not go all the way, but there was no shot that was going to last. I was a hair trigger away from losing control every time we were together, and soon, this flesh and blood would fail me. Before that happened, I had to have some idea of where things were going from here.

On a whim, I told Cullen to go on ahead of me. "I'm going to stop off and grab a coffee. See you up there."

He was already distracted by a text he'd gotten and threw up a quick wave before disappearing through the double doors.

I veered off toward the little café next door and ordered one of those mocha lattes Evie liked and a chocolate-covered biscotti.

It was totally irrational how excited I felt as I stepped off the elevator to our offices a few minutes later and made a beeline toward Evie's desk. She was on the phone but she waved at me, a smile playing on her lips.

"Yes, Linda. I totally understand. And I agree, the purple would look great with the green, so for the next round of images, that's what we'll do."

I set the coffee on Evie's desk and tugged the biscotti out of the bag. Her whole face lit up, and her fingers brushed mine as she took it from me.

"You're my hero," she mouthed, her eyes going soft with something I couldn't quite name.

I went to my desk feeling like exactly that. A fucking superhero, to be exact. What was it about this woman that she could make me feel that way with something as simple as a smile?

I thought back to a time when we were younger that I'd seen that same smile.

A bunch of us had gone swimming at the lake one hot summer day. I'd been with a girl, Annalise Benson. She'd developed early, and I was ashamed now to say that was all I'd seen in her, because she was also catty and a total snob.

That day at the lake, we'd been dating for about a month, and I still hadn't been able to see past her tits. Evie had been around twelve and had finally started to grow out of her tattletale stage, so we'd let her come with us. She was paddling around in the water while Cullen chatted with some friends on the beach.

Annalise and I were making out in the shallows when I heard Evie cry out. I'd pulled away so fast, I nearly knocked Annalise on her ass to get over to Evie. She'd apparently cut her heel on a sharp rock and was bleeding badly enough to require stitches.

As I'd carried her to shore, I overheard Annalise muttering under her breath. "I don't know why we had to bring that clumsy brat with us, anyway."

I could feel Evie stiffen in my arms at the cruel words, and as I looked into her tear-filled eyes, an icy rage had flowed through me.

"We didn't have to bring her. We wanted to," I'd snapped. "And she might be clumsy, but at least she's not a stuck-up bitch."

Annalise had taken off in a huff, taking my chances of getting laid along with her, but I didn't give a shit. Because Evie had looked up at me with that smile.

Why had it taken so long for me to see what I saw in her now?

And how the fuck was I going to explain all this to her brother in a way that didn't tear us all apart?

Chapter Twenty

Evie

Who would ever compare?

That's what I found myself thinking as I sneaked a peek at Smith out of the corner of my eye. He was focused on the road, his profile superhero clean, his strong, capable hands on the wheel, a small smile playing about his firm mouth.

If it was just his looks, maybe I could have dealt. Looks weren't everything, after all. But it wasn't just that. The past weeks had been magical. He made me laugh, he made me come, he made me feel important and grown-up, and best of all? He made me feel heard. When I spoke, he didn't sit there texting on his phone like a lot of the guys my age did. He looked at me and he really listened, his phone nowhere in sight.

I shifted in the passenger's seat and held back a sigh. This was exactly why I'd made the whole casual edict so adamantly in the first place. Not for Smith. Smith was all about casual. In fact, I was pretty sure he'd never done anything *but* casual aside from one long-term girlfriend, and even after they'd broken up, he certainly hadn't shed any tears.

No, the casual label was for me. I'd hoped that the more I said it, the more I could remind myself that this was all temporary.

Every last bit of it.

The sweet dates, and even sweeter kisses. Having Smith's undivided attention. Feeling his hands . . . and mouth on me. And when it was over, things were going to have to go back to the way they were.

I was a smart cookie. Surely, just like memorizing state capitals, if I repeated it often enough, it would stick.

But apparently, the line between my brain and my heart was out of order, because while my rational mind accepted the inevitable outcome, my heart was on a whole other level. Filled with hope and anticipation and excitement. It was making plans and promises, and daydreaming about babies.

Stupid fucking heart.

My throat ached and my eyes burned with pre-emptive grief. Funny, I'd always been the careful one, and the one time I took a risk . . .

There was no question about it. This one was going to leave a mark. A long-lasting, indelible scar on my heart.

Exactly, dummy. And there's no changing it now. What's done is done, so you might as well enjoy it while you've got it.

Resolved to do exactly that, I shoved aside my melancholy and glanced out the window, watching trees flash by.

"Where are we going, anyway?" I asked, straightening in my seat and shooting Smith a questioning glance.

Our past dates, I'd typically met him somewhere away from our usual hangouts so we wouldn't get spotted together, but tonight, Smith had insisted on picking me up. Now, though, I realized we were headed north toward somewhere outside the city. There was nothing this way but houses and churches.

"We'll be there in about sixty seconds, and then you'll see," he said, his half smile ramping up to full power.

That smile was like being kissed by the sun, warming me through to my core, and I realized I didn't give a crap where our date was, as long as I was with Smith.

He pulled down a cul-de-sac and into the driveway of a modest but cozy-looking house I'd never seen before.

"I probably should've warned you to wear an old shirt, but I'll buy you a new one if this turns out the way I think it will."

It was only then that I realized that he was dressed super casual himself. A hoodie and a pair of worn jeans as opposed to my new sweater and high-heeled boots combo. Now my curiosity amped up to code red, and I gaped at him.

"What the heck is going on, Smith? Are we meeting some friends of yours for a double date or something?" *And if so, wouldn't that news get back to my brother?*

But I kept that last part to myself because I realized with a start that I *wanted* to meet Smith's friends. I wanted to know everything about him. Become part of his life story for real instead of just a note in the margins. The melancholy threatened to return like a gray cloud, but I pushed it away again.

Whatever tomorrow brought, tonight I was with a guy I wanted, I liked, and I trusted. So tonight? I was going to take happiness by the balls and squeeze out every last drop.

"I don't think I'd call it a double date, exactly, but . . ."

He trailed off as the front door swung open and Smith's older sister Pam came charging out in a wrinkled dress, running a brush through her hair as she went. I'd never been one to run in heels, but Pam was wild-eyed and sprinting like the devil himself was on her heels. Her husband, Tim, who I'd only seen in pictures, followed behind, grinning broadly.

Smith motioned for me to step out of the car. I did, and he followed suit.

"You guys. I can't even tell you how much this means to me right now. Like—" Pam broke off, her eyes filling with tears as she clutched my forearms. "I thank you. My husband thanks you. My sanity thanks you." She dragged me in for a hug and then pulled away. "I'd love to stay and chat, but I've got to go before Winnie notices I left." She shot a fearful glance over her shoulder and then dashed toward the passenger's side of the minivan in the driveway, blowing Smith a kiss from afar. "Love you, bro. You're the best. And you have my number. But don't, like, use it unless someone is literally on fire."

Tim chuckled and ran a hand through his red hair, making it stand up on end as he gave Smith a hearty slap on the shoulder. "Finn has decided that sleep is for quitters, Mac just projectile shat on the dress Pam had started out wearing, and Winnie flushed Pam's bracelet down the toilet. We need a break so bad, my man. We are forever in your debt."

"Tim! Christ, please frigging hurry before they see us," Pam hissed before turning her gaze toward Smith and me. "And you two, hustle on inside. They've been alone for forty-seven seconds. They could have already booby-trapped the place by now, so enter at your own risk."

The minivan doors slammed shut and the vehicle's tires actually squealed as they back out.

Smith turned my way and his grin faltered a little as he took in my shell-shocked expression.

"Okay, so I know this looks bad. But I swear, they're exaggerating a little. If you're miserable, I won't be mad if you call an Uber to take you home, and you can pick the next date, all right?"

I gnawed on my lower lip, blinking hard to keep the tears burning the back of my lids from falling. How could I possibly explain how I was feeling without scaring the hell out of him?

I'm not crying because I want to leave. I'm crying because I've never wanted to be anywhere more than I want to be here with you, right now.

Instead, I mustered a smile and settled for, "Are you kidding me? Kids are a blast. We're going to have a great time. Let's do this." Then I let my mouth pull up into the smile I'd been trying to keep in.

Smith looked so relieved, the vice grip on my heart loosened a little, and I chuckled.

"Although, between you and your sister, I gotta tell you, I'm half expecting these kids to be swinging from the chandeliers, so let's head inside," I added.

He rounded the car and popped open the trunk,

tugging out a bag before closing it.

"Don't be scared. They're not so bad. They're what we like to call *spirited*." He closed the distance between us and took my hand. "Come on. Let's get inside so I can introduce you to the wrecking crew."

The next few minutes went by in a frantic blur. Copper-haired Winnie introduced herself to me and then promptly brandished a foam sword and demanded that I get my sword "or die a miserable death!" while Finn slugged me in the crotch with a Nerf gun.

While I was defending myself from that onslaught, Smith had dropped his bag in order to chase baby Mac, who in the short time that we'd been outside with Pam and Tim had decided that the diaper life wasn't for him anymore. He was tearing around the living room buck naked, his plump little baby buns jiggling for all the world to see. And damn if he didn't make dimpled butt cheeks look cute. It was a look I wished I could pull off.

And through it all, I hadn't stopped grinning. I couldn't have wished for a better date. Because, casual be damned, Smith had let me in. The love he felt for his niece and nephews was so plain to see, it was etched into his every feature.

I'd met his sister Pam a few times when I was younger, just because our brothers had spent so much time together, but this was different. Smith had brought me here to spend time with the people in his life who mattered most to him.

It might not mean anything, Evie. He could have just forgotten that he'd promised to babysit, and you got folded into the mix.

But, damn it, it *felt* like it meant something. It felt like it meant . . . everything.

"Do you want to have a tea party with me?" Winnie asked, dropping her sword and eyeing me speculatively.

I nodded and squatted to meet her at eye level. "Of course. Who wouldn't want to have a tea party?"

She jerked her chin toward baby Mac, who was still diaperless and was currently attempting to ride the dog. "Macky hates tea parties. All he wants to do is poop and eat Cheerios." She rolled her eyes and gave me a conspiratorial grin. "Babies."

"I'm going to order pizza," Smith said, finally getting

a handle on a squirming Mac and tucking him under his arm like a football. "What do you want on yours?"

"M&M'S," Finn piped up. "And pineapple."

Smith made a gagging noise and ruffled Finn's hair. "I'm going to have to veto the candy on there because it's both sacrilege and disgusting, plus your mother would kill me. But the pineapple is a go."

Finn nodded, his face solemn. "I accept that compromise so long as we can have some of the M&M'S from that bag you brought when it's movie time."

Smith barked out a laugh. "How do you know there are M&M'S in there?"

"He always brings M&M'S," Winnie whispered, cupping her hand to my ear in order to protect her secret.

I couldn't help but smile, equally in awe of the man as the kiddos were. Seeing him in action like that, watching him navigate this situation with humor and ease, was fascinating.

As the night progressed, Smith and I had zero time alone together, but it was right up there with one of the best nights of my life. The kids had boundless energy, and the life and laughter in this little house was everything a family should be. I soaked it in like a sponge, committing it all to memory. Every uninhibited childish guffaw, every baby squeal of delight, every mess, and every hug.

By the time ten p.m. rolled around, the pizza boxes were empty, the kids were sprawled out across Smith and me on the couch, and I was on cloud nine. Glowing from the inside out, exhausted, but happier than I could ever remember being.

"Thank you," I murmured softly, running my index finger through Mac's feathery blond hair and shooting Smith a watery smile. "Thank you so much for inviting me. They're amazing."

He nodded and reached out to tuck a strand of hair behind my ear. "So are you. They're nuts about you."

I wish you could be nuts about me too, I wanted to whisper. But I held it in and tucked it away deep in my heart.

Life could be a grind sometimes, but tonight had been a rare gem. An oasis of perfection. No way was I going to ruin it.

He leaned in, past baby Mac and over little Winnie, and pressed a soft, gentle kiss to my mouth. As his tongue swept across mine, I said a little prayer.

Come on, Smith. Just give me one chance . . . . and maybe a little hope that we can make this real.

Chapter Twenty-One

Smith

"I love those kids."

I could still hear the warmth in Evie's voice as she watched Pam's little monsters running around like lunatics as they played indoor tag.

After the night we'd had, most women would have left, shell-shocked and ready to have their tubes tied. A few might have stuck it out with a grin-and-bear-it attitude. But I was pretty sure almost none of them would have joined in and wound up covered in s'mores under a pile of exhausted little bodies at the end of the night.

Evie hadn't put up with it, or done it to humor me. Her cheeks had glowed with pleasure, and her lips had been tilted up in a perma-smile. By the time I'd dropped her off at the end of the night, she'd been sporting a pair of crooked braids courtesy of little Winnie, and an electric-purple manicure that covered almost as much of her fingers as it did her nails, but I'll be damned if she'd ever looked more beautiful to me.

My brain instantly supplied an image of her in that peach lace teddy, and I found myself grinning. Okay, so maybe it was a tie.

The thing that was becoming clearer by the day was exactly how much I enjoyed Evie's company. Whether she was writhing against me, begging me to make her come, or belly laughing beside me as we watched a movie, she'd managed to work herself into the very fabric of my life.

And I liked it.

I waited for the feeling that always followed that realization. The fight-or-flight response that made me do something stupid to fuck things up, or cut bait and walk away. But cool, never-get-attached Smith was dead silent. Maybe he was dead altogether, because all I felt was hope and excitement for the future. Anticipation of more nights like the one we'd spent with Pam's kids.

Maybe with our own kids someday?

I gulped down a mouthful of now-tepid coffee, then set the empty mug in the sink.

As crazy as it would have seemed a month ago, now the thought of having some rug rats of my own—rug rats with Evie Reed—didn't seem crazy at all.

Which meant it was long past time to make an honest man of myself and talk to Cullen. Whatever the outcome, it had to be better than Evie and me sneaking around like a pair of star-crossed teenagers. Cullen was a grown man. He'd be pissed at first, but he'd come around. And then I could finally make this right. I could finally have Evie like I'd dreamed about.

I thumbed through my contacts and tapped Cullen's number, my muscles tense as I waited for him to pick up.

"What's up, man?"

He was slightly out of breath, and I glanced at my watch. Eight a.m.

"You already running?" I asked, striving to keep my tone light.

"Nope, just did shoulders at the gym and am about to hit the pavement. Want to join?" he asked.

Seemed like the running trail was as good a place as any to get into this shit. And, hey, at least we'd be close to the lake in the event he straight-up murdered me and needed an easy place to hide the body. After all the lies I'd told him, the least I could do was make it convenient for him.

"Yep, I'm in," I said. "Meet you by the flagpole in fifteen."

I was chill as ice cream as I changed into my gym pants and laced up my kicks, but by the time I reached our designated meeting place, my heart was hammering a drumbeat against my ribs. The cadence felt oddly like the lyrics to a song with only one word.

Trai-tor.

Trai-tor.

Trai-tor.

"What's up, asshole?" Cullen jogged up behind me and punched my shoulder lightly.

I managed a grin in spite of the dark cloud hanging over me. "Hey, prick."

"Glad you called," he said. "We haven't hung out in a while."

Guilt weighed down my stomach, and suddenly the last thing I felt like doing was running, but I sure as shit couldn't back out now.

"Yeah, been busy," I muttered, following his lead and doing a few perfunctory stretches.

"That's okay. Today's my five-mile day, so we've got plenty of time to catch up," he replied with an evil grin. "Ready, chump?"

Shit.

I'd been banking on the whole run plus a cooldown taking thirty minutes, tops. I had it all planned out in my head. Ten minutes of bullshit, another ten spent on work stuff, and then, just when he was starting to get short of breath, I'd test the waters on the whole Evie thing.

Short and sweet.

Best of all, if things didn't go the way I hoped, we wouldn't be stuck running next to each other, stewing and pissed off. He could go his way, I could go mine, and he'd have the rest of the weekend to cool off.

Five miles from soup to nuts was going to take at

least forty-five minutes, maybe even closer to an hour. We hadn't even started yet, and already that length of time felt interminable.

Lies will do that to you, you jackass.

"Yup, let's rock and roll," I said with a grim nod.

We took off at an easy jog, letting our muscles warm up and getting into the groove. Cullen chattered about a blind date he'd gone on that went horribly wrong, and I found myself having to slow my pace because I was laughing so hard.

"A lot of people have pictures of themselves in their apartments, Cull. I have a couple of me and you hiking, and that fishing trip—"

"No, see, that's what I mean," he said, shooting me an incredulous look over his shoulder as he jogged. "These weren't group shots. It was literally just dozens of pictures of herself with her cats on every available surface. They were everywhere. In some, she was looking over one shoulder, like old-style glamour shots, and in others, she was leaning her chin on her hand looking off into the distance. So when I mentioned that she sure had a lot of pictures of herself, you know what she said?"

I shook my head, waiting for the punch line.

"She said, 'If I don't love myself, how is anyone else going to love me?'"

I chuckled and sprinted toward him to catch up again. "Isn't that like a Dr. Phil quote or some shit?"

"It is. In fact, I'm pretty sure ninety percent of the things she said to me were Dr. Phil quotes. It was bizarre. But to top it all off, when I left, she said, 'I don't usually do this on the first date, but I really like you,' and she kissed my forehead, like she was my great aunt or some shit. I'm telling you, bro, she was whacked."

"So, when are you going to see her again?" I quipped.

He threw his head back and laughed. "Actually, I gave her your number. Hope that's cool?"

As we wound our way around the lake, I couldn't help but feel that twinge of nostalgia creeping in. Cullen really was like a brother to me, and I missed this. But since I'd started spending time with Evie, my own guilt over the situation made it almost painful to be around him. It was definitely time to tear off this fucking Band-Aid.

"Sounds like that's one for the books," I said lightly. "Speaking of dating, anything going on with your sister in that department? Been a long time since she's had a boyfriend. Last one I recall was in high school, and even that was barely a thing."

Cullen shot me a puzzled look and shrugged. "No clue. I don't ask her about that shit. Mainly because I'm afraid she'll actually tell me. You don't get it because Pam is older, I guess, but it's weird thinking about your little sister . . ." He trailed off and let out a disgusted growl. "You know what I mean."

"I hear you," I muttered, resisting the urge to change the subject and abort this clusterfuck of a mission altogether.

Suck it up, asshole.

There were only two options here. Tell him, or end it with Evie. Somehow in the past few weeks, option number two was no longer on the table.

I drew in a breath and let loose the first sally. "She's a

twenty-two-year-old woman, Cullen. She's got to grow up sometime. Don't you want to see her find a good guy and settle down? Maybe have a family someday?"

His reply came back without hesitation. "Nope."

Guilt gave way to irritation, and I scowled at him. "That's a little ridiculous, don't you think?"

His gait faltered as he turned his head to stare at me. "No, I don't *think*. And I'm trying to figure out why the fuck you're asking me this shit right now."

I slowed, and suddenly the sound of his feet pounding the dirt beside me stopped.

Jesus, this was going to suck.

I stopped and turned to face him. He stood, his hands loosely on his hips, but there was nothing casual about his expression.

"You got something to tell me, Smith?"

The anger was already there, bubbling right beneath the surface. As much as I hated being the target of it, this conversation had been an eye-opener, and I knew now more than ever it was the right thing to do, no matter how ugly it got.

His eyes were trained on my face, his jaw clenched as he pressed. "Why all the questions, Smith?"

"Asking for a friend?" I shot back with a smirk, one last attempt to bring things down a notch and keep it light. But Cullen was having no part of it.

"I can't even believe you're thinking about this. She's twenty-two. She's practically a fucking kid," he snapped, pacing now like a caged lion. Then he stopped in his tracks, his cheeks going chalk white. "Are you fucking her already?" he demanded in a whisper that somehow felt shittier than if he'd shouted it at me.

"No."

It felt inhumane to add the caveat—*not yet, at least*—but there was no question it hung in the air between us like a poisonous smog.

"You son of a bitch," he snarled, his fist clenching open and closed.

His eyes were wild with anger and something like betrayal, but before I could apologize, he was stalking toward me. He stopped just a few inches from my face.

"If you were anyone else, I'd beat the living shit out of you right now. Instead, I'm going to take you at your word that you haven't slept with her and give you a chance to try and undo this shit. Stop now and nothing has to change. We can work together, and once I get over the fact that you went behind my back and even considered this shit, we can probably go back to being friends. But that's if and only if you agree to shut it down." His nostrils flared as he glared at me. "Now."

We were friends. The best. But Evie was a person. A woman in her own right with thoughts and feelings and free will of her own. The fact that Cullen was talking about her like she was some antiquated piece of the Reed family property made my blood hum with fury.

I hated that it had come to this, and there was no denying it was my bad, but my anger got the better of me and I shoved him hard in the chest.

"First of all, I wasn't asking your permission," I muttered. "I was trying to break some news to you in the right way. Granted, I should've told you sooner, but this macho asshole bullshit of yours doesn't exactly make it easy, and your sister asked me not to."

The heat of his outrage burned beneath the surface. "You got a lot of nerve telling m—"

"Second of all," I cut in, jabbing a finger in his direction. "Evie is a twenty-two-year-old without any love life on the horizon, probably in part because of you. You were like her hulking shadow, and guys were afraid to even get near her in high school. You think that's healthy?" I demanded, pissed off and on a roll now. "She needs space to grow and learn about life. Keeping her close so you can protect her is selfish, Cullen. How is she ever going to learn from her mistakes, or fall and pick herself back up if she's never allowed to make any?"

Cullen snorted in disgust and crossed his arms over his chest. "And what? You want that first big mistake to be you?" He let out a low laugh. "I know you, man. You haven't had a serious relationship since Karen, and even that wound up being a royal fuckup. What makes you think you're good enough for my sister?"

It was a question I'd asked myself more than once in the past few weeks, and I didn't have a good answer to it yet. But I knew one thing for sure. It wasn't going to stop me from trying.

"Luckily, that's not for either of us to decide. That's Evie's decision, isn't it?" I said, cold fury settling over me. "If that seems out of line and you want to fire me or whatever, then go ahead."

I could have told him that I'd changed. I could have told him that what I felt for Evie was different, but that wasn't the point. Even if I hadn't, she still had the right to decide her path in life without worrying about her brother's approval.

Cullen's face was stony as he stared me down in silence. "It's like that, then?" he muttered finally, his legs moving once again and he started past me. "You know your way back. I don't want to see your fucking face right now."

I watched him until he was out of sight, half expecting him to turn around and come back. He didn't, and I took off running the way we'd come, pushing myself to my limit in hopes of burning off some of this adrenaline.

That hadn't gone well. I'd known it wouldn't, but at

some point during our familiar banter on the run, there had been a brief second—a tiny kernel of hope—that maybe it would turn out better than I'd imagined.

It wasn't until I got back to my apartment bathed in sweat, my muscles shaking with fatigue, that I realized I hadn't called Evie yet to tell her what I'd done.

Damn it, I should have warned her.

I sank down on the couch and said a silent prayer that I hadn't lost both Reeds today.

Chapter Twenty-Two

Evie

Little white candles flickered on the coffee table, and soft jazz floated through the air. Smith's apartment was spotlessly clean, complete with neat rows of vacuum lines in the carpet. Two wineglasses and a bottle of chilled pinot grigio sat beside a plate holding a single slice of pound cake with fluffy whipped cream.

When Smith had invited me over tonight, I'd told him I had dinner plans with Maggie I didn't want to break, and so he invited me for dessert instead.

"What's all this?" My gaze cut over to Smith, who was standing beside the sofa smirking.

He shrugged. "Just a little token to say how much I've enjoyed spending time together."

My real question, the one that I couldn't voice was—
is tonight the *night?*

After our last conversation, I wasn't sure if Smith had talked to my brother, and honestly, I didn't want to know.

I wanted to remain blissfully in the dark. The only thing I cared about was that we were together, and the sizzle of electricity that flowed between us was swamping all my other senses.

"Sit. Make yourself comfortable," Smith said.

I lowered myself to the sofa while he uncorked the wine and poured us each a glass.

"Cheers." I clinked my glass to his, butterflies dancing in my belly.

"To do-overs," he whispered, a smile playing at the edges of his full mouth.

We each took a sip, and the cool, crisp wine slid down my throat, warming my insides.

Smith leaned closer and reached out to tuck a lock of hair behind my ear. The look in his gaze was intense, heated, passionate, and I had to bite my tongue to keep from admitting how much I wanted him.

"You're beautiful, Everleigh," he whispered. "Always have been."

My face heating under his careful scrutiny, I did the

only thing I could think to do. I leaned into his touch, my eyes falling closed as his lips met mine.

His kiss was so careful, so controlled. He nipped at my lips, gently pressing his mouth to mine, until I took his lower lip between mine and gave it a sharp bite.

He pulled back, fire blazing in his gaze as his tongue traced the abused spot. "It's going to be like that, huh?"

Swallowing down my nerves, I knew what I wanted tonight. We'd been building toward this moment since Paris, and only a natural disaster was going to stop me.

After setting both of our wineglasses on the table, I climbed into his lap, then brought my mouth to his neck. I didn't need words to show him what I wanted. I rocked my hips against his, and found his cock was as hard as steel already.

Gripping my ass in his palms, Smith pulled me closer. The wine and dessert and romance were forgotten. Our rising lust demanded attention.

"What do you want?" he murmured between stolen kisses.

"Everything," I moaned, my lips brushing his as I spoke.

"That's a dangerous thing to say to a man." Smith's hands roamed up my sides until he reached my bra, his fingertips lightly teasing me.

"You've given me pleasure, gotten me off . . ." I licked my lips, meeting his eyes. "But I never got to return the favor."

His eyes stayed locked on mine as I slid from the couch to my knees in front of him.

"Tonight I intend to change that."

"Are you saying you want your mouth on my cock, Everleigh?" His tone was steady, but the deep hoarseness to his voice told me that was an idea he was very much okay with.

I reached for the button to his jeans, but he pushed my hand away.

"Put your hands behind your back. Be a good girl." Smith's playful side was back, and it had me clenching my thighs together.

I obeyed, lacing my fingers together behind my back, and watched in fascination as he dragged down the zipper to his pants.

Smith tugged down his pants and boxers, freeing the most beautiful male appendage I'd ever laid eyes on.

Our brief encounter in the hotel had been entirely in the dark. The desire to strip him naked and see every inch of his muscled skin raced through me. I'd never been filled with such blazing-hot desire in my entire life.

His large hand circled the base of his shaft and he stroked slowly up the length of it, stopping at the end, where his thumb captured a drop of fluid, smoothing it over the wide tip.

"Is this what you want?" he growled.

Transfixed by his erotic show, I opened my mouth to speak but nothing came out. I nodded my head instead.

"Come here, baby doll."

Leaning in, I reached for his cock, but Smith made a noise of disapproval in his throat.

"Naughty girl. Keep your hands behind your back.

You told me this was about taking me in your mouth."

My gaze flashed on his, and the challenge I saw in his hazel eyes lit a fuse inside me.

"Open," he said.

I did, bringing my mouth toward his lap where he placed the head of his cock against my tongue.

Treating him to a leisurely open-mouthed kiss, I dragged my tongue along his silken flesh, loving the way I heard his breath hitch when I did something he liked.

We continued like that, with him feeding his hot length to me, inch by delicious inch. The wetness between my legs was impossible to ignore as my desire burned brighter.

I opened my mouth, releasing him with a soft sucking noise. "I need to touch you."

"You are touching me. And it feels fucking amazing, I should add."

"No, I need to take you in my hands."

He petted my cheek with his thumb, his gaze full of

sexy mischief. "If that's what you want." Then he released his cock so that it rested on his belly, and gestured for me to go ahead.

I began tentatively at first, touching him carefully, grazing my fingertips across his taut skin.

"You're not going to break me," he said on a groan, the sound filled with frustrated need.

Enjoying the weight of his manhood in my palm, I pumped my fist along the entire length of him, massaging his balls with my other hand.

He was well-endowed, and I wanted to savor every hot inch of him. Working his length with my fist, I brought my mouth to him again, sucking, licking, and kissing him as I caressed.

As he stroked my cheek possessively, his eyes stayed glued to my mouth and where his cock was sliding in and out between my parted lips.

A deep groan of satisfaction tore from his mouth. "Jesus, Everleigh." He cursed under his breath, his fist tightening on the couch beside his thigh.

Part of me couldn't believe I was doing this to *Smith*. He'd always been my older brother's hot, hunky friend, and completely off-limits. And now here he was with his big cock buried deep in my throat, making grunting noises whenever I swallowed him all the way. My insides clenched violently.

"That's enough." Smith pulled away suddenly, rising to his feet and tugging me up with him. "I'm not going to come in your mouth tonight . . . as much as I might want to."

Chapter Twenty-Three

Smith

My cock was so hard, I wondered if it might explode before I ever really got inside her. But then there she was, buck naked on my bed and spread before me, and I didn't wonder anything more at all.

"You're so fucking sexy," I said, my voice harsh and low. It was finally happening, and so far, it was beyond anything I'd imagined.

And, God damn, had I imagined. All those long, sleepless nights remembering Evie exactly this way that first time at the hotel in the instant before I'd shoved the sheet over her and looked away. That memory had been seared into my mind forever. Only now I had a new one to prop right by its side.

Hopefully, the first of many.

Her cheeks were pink as she held out her arms. "Are you getting in, or are you going to leave me here all alone?"

"Oh, hell yeah, I'm getting in. And you'll be begging me to leave you alone by the time I'm done," I murmured, sliding into the bed next to her and resting my hand low on her belly. She shivered at my touch, goose bumps breaking out over her creamy skin.

"So soft," I said, trailing my fingers up past her belly button and higher, until I palmed the heavy weight of her breast in my hand. A low hum escaped her lips as I bent my head low, capturing one hard nipple between my teeth and nipping it gently.

"Smith . . ."

Her voice was breathy, full of need, and it sent a white-hot bolt of lust slicing through me. My cock pulsed and swelled as I traced my tongue in a circle before tugging her nipple into my mouth to suck in earnest.

"Mmm, Smith . . ."

Her breasts were so sensitive that I made a mental note to see if I could make her come just from playing with them.

Next time.

Because this time? We weren't stopping until we fucked the lights out in this place.

I breathed in deep, inhaling her light, sexy scent as I sent my free hand on a scouting mission. Down her flat tummy again and lower, until I cupped that hot, wet pussy. She arched into my touch, sending two of my fingers slipping over that creamy slit and making me groan in the process.

Ladies first, Smith, and don't you fucking forget it.

But my brain went on sabbatical as she extended her leg and ground her toned thigh against my cock. The pressure was enough to make my ears ring, and I squeezed my eyes closed to get some relief.

It was all too much. She was coming at me from every direction, setting all of my senses ablaze at once. The taste of her skin against my tongue, the feel of her smooth, tight cunt in my hand, the sound of her choppy, broken breath. This had been a long time coming, and if I didn't pull back, it was going to be over before we even started.

I angled my cock away from her thigh with a groan

and released her nipple. "Lay back and spread your legs wider for me, baby," I whispered.

Her gaze was molten hot as she wet her lips and did exactly as I'd asked, baring herself to me completely.

For a second, I just took in the view. My hand seated between Evie's thighs, my glossy fingers stroking her up and down. With a growl, I massaged her swollen clit with my thumb and a tremor ran through her. She might technically still be a newbie at this, but by now, I knew what she needed. I knew her body and exactly how to wring pleasure from it. Her hips were moving in maddening circles, urging me on as I sank my fingers deeper into her waiting heat.

"Yeah, just like that," she moaned, tossing her head slowly against the pillow.

I swallowed hard and pressed in deeper, sliding two fingers fully inside her now even as my thumb worked that bundle of nerves in slow circles.

"That feel good to you, Everleigh?" I demanded hoarsely, loving the sound of her cries, wanting to pull more of them from her mouth. "You want my cock right here?" I asked, plunging my fingers into her until she whimpered my name.

Her cries had become incoherent, and her chest was heaving as she thrust toward me, urging me to work her harder . . . faster. She was close, so close, and I couldn't wait to feel her go over the edge.

I pressed my face between her thighs and replaced my thumb with my tongue, nibbling on her clit until she clawed at my shoulders in an unspoken plea. In answer, I sucked the tiny nub of flesh into my mouth and drew hard, once . . . twice, and then she screamed.

My cock jerked, and I arched into the mattress to keep from coming as her orgasm rained down on me. Coating my fingers even as her pussy clamped over them like a vice.

"Smith, oh God!"

I held it together, just barely, as she shook beneath me, but I was one false move from exploding myself. The moment the last tremors faded, I climbed up the bed and scrambled for a condom.

Seconds later, with a tear of foil and a quick fumble, I

was ready. I pressed her back against the pillow and stroked her flushed cheek with my fingertip, my heart nearly as full as my aching cock.

"You ready?" I asked softly.

Her eyes gleamed and she nodded. "I've never been more ready for anything in my life."

I gripped my cock and slid between her legs, resting the head against her opening. Her bottom lip quivered as I brushed a lock of hair away from her face.

Once I was in, I was in. There was no way I could live with myself if I had no intention of being with Evie beyond today, not even to satisfy her virginity vendetta. That thought only made me more eager to get inside her, though, because I'd never been more sure in my life.

But maybe this was just a box to check for her. Once she'd had a proper, satisfying sexual experience, would that be it?

For me, it was so much more. As I looked into her eyes and thrust inside her, filling her . . . taking her, it all seemed so fucking clear.

I was in love. I wanted Evie Reed to be mine now and forever. Now, it was up to her what happened after tonight.

So you better make it good, Hamilton.

Her mouth dropped open in a silent gasp as I drove forward, slow and steady. Inch by excruciating inch.

"God, you're fucking tight," I bit out through gritted teeth.

"Sorry," she whispered.

But for once, she didn't look sorry, or shy, or nervous. She looked totally enthralled.

Good start.

I was seated about halfway when I felt it again. The feeling that had put my radar on high alert that night in the hotel. The band of muscles wrapping around my cock like a fist. This was the tricky bit. I needed to move forward to finish the deed, but getting into her tight little pussy that deep would come at a price—my sanity.

I closed my eyes and sucked in a steadying breath before opening them again. "Relax," I whispered.

She nodded furiously, her throat working as she swallowed hard. "Trying to."

It was easy to forget she'd done this before. Both because I wanted to pretend that I was the first one to claim her, and also because whoever she'd been with must have been hung like a fucking field mouse.

I inched forward, and her every muscle tensed against me. "Tell me if I hurt you, baby. Don't want that."

"N-no. Not exactly. It feels huge," she whispered, flicking out her tongue to lap at the beads of sweat dotting her upper lip. "Like pressure, but good too, you know?"

I bit back a groan. I did know. If there was any more pressure on my cock and balls right now, I'd literally disintegrate.

"One more push and I'll be all the way in, okay?"

She nodded, and her eyes fluttered shut. "Yup."

I leaned down to kiss her softly on the mouth. Then balancing onto my forearms, I drove forward in a single smooth motion until my cock was fully seated deep inside her. My vision went hazy as her gasp rang out in the silent room.

I wanted to stay still. To give her time to adjust, and ask her again if she was all right. But the weeks of denying my need finally exploded inside me, and I was all instinct.

"I'm sorry," I muttered, my hips pounding against her now of their own accord. Heat snaked up my shaft, and my cock bucked as I realized with a rush of relief that she was moving beneath me, her own soft hips crashing against mine.

"For what?" she breathed.

"Being too rough with you." I clenched my teeth, my ass muscles flexing as I pumped harder.

"Feels so good. Don't stop."

Her whimpers became shouts as I filled her again and again, plowing forward until I hit bottom, her channel working me over in a sensual assault.

"I'm going to come," she groaned, her fingernails tearing into my shoulders.

"Fuck, yeah. Come for me, Evie." The headboard slammed against the wall in a steady rhythm as she shattered around me.

"Smith!"

Thank God.

Evie's back bowed, her breasts smashing against my chest as she came. She clutched my ass, melding her body to mine, dragging me over the edge with her.

"Fuck."

My muscles clenched as heat thundered through me. Her gaze locked with mine as I unloaded inside her, coming so hard, I almost blacked out. I flexed my hips, drawing out our pleasure, pressing deeper and holding true until the last wave subsided. Then I collapsed on top of her with a groan.

"Boy, when you finally do it, you do it right," I murmured in her ear.

Her breathy laugh warmed my neck, and she pressed a kiss to my shoulder. "All credit to you, good sir. It makes me really glad it was you, Smith."

It wasn't until she said the words that I realized how much it meant to me that she felt that way.

I rolled to the side, tugging her with me as I went, and tucked her under my arm. "I'm glad it was me too, Evie."

She was totally right. You could have a do-over. No one could take this from us. It was perfect.

We lay there for a long time in each other's arms, totally silent, just soaking in the warm glow. I almost could have fallen into a light sleep until I felt her soft lips graze my ear.

"It felt like that was a good start, but there's so many more questions I have," she murmured, her soft hand traveling down my abs slowly until my cock leaped up to meet her.

"Looks like you've come to the right place," I growled, grabbing her by the hips and yanking her on top of me.

Her squeal of laughter rang through me like a song, and I pulled her mouth down to mine.

Tomorrow, we'd talk it all through, and I'd find out if her heart was in the same place as mine.

Tonight?

I just wanted to make her scream again.

Chapter Twenty-Four

Evie

The room was too warm. That was the first thing I realized as I blinked open hazy eyes. The second thing I realized was that I was butt naked and sprawled out over Smith's body.

As I scrambled off him into a sitting position, my body ached in places I had never ached before.

"Evie?" Smith's sleepy voice asked.

Rubbing my eyes, I looked at the digital clock and saw it was just past midnight. We'd made love twice and then had fallen asleep in each other's arms.

"Be right back," I whispered, climbing from the bed. Padding naked and barefoot into the adjoining bathroom, I flipped on the light and sank onto the toilet to relieve myself.

After washing my hands, I tiptoed back into the bedroom. Smith was lying quiet and still in the center of the bed, the sheet draped over his waist. My throat tightened as I watched his chest rise and fall in a steady rhythm.

This night was everything I'd dreamed it could be. It had been the most amazing sexual experience of my life, and Smith had been the perfect man to share it with. He was so attentive, so giving and loving, and I'd been completely lost in the moment. But now? Now I was freaking out a bit.

Feeling around on the floor, I located my underwear and jeans, and slid them on. My bra was hanging off the back of a chair, and my shirt was nowhere to be found.

Exiting the bedroom as quietly as I could, I headed for the living room and spotted my shirt on the hallway floor.

The need to be in my own space outweighed everything. I had to process what had happened tonight and my growing feelings for Smith. And I needed to do it in the safety of my own home.

I'd grown closer to Smith in these past few weeks than I'd ever imagined was possible. It was no longer just about sex. Yes, we'd had an amazing time between the sheets, and I was sure no man would ever compare, but things were so much more complicated than that. He'd let me into his life, introduced me to his lovable yet chaotic family, shown me what it was like to let go and have fun.

And now that it was over? I was more heartbroken than I'd ever imagined.

Dressing quickly, I slipped on my shoes and coat, scratched out a quick note, and fled.

• • •

Pushing open the heavy glass door to the office Monday morning, I forced my mouth into a smile. "Morning," I said to my brother.

"Hey, Evie," Cullen said, his eyes still trained on his computer screen. "Is there a reason you're"—his gaze dropped to his wristwatch—"forty minutes late?"

I sniffed. I'd been frozen in fear this morning, sure that my brother would read guilt and heartache all over me. "Sorry about that. I'm not feeling very well today."

His gaze swung over to mine and softened. "If you need to go home and take it easy today, it's no big deal."

I nodded. "Thanks."

We worked in silence for a few minutes until I couldn't help but ask the question burning a hole in my brain. "Where's Smith? Did he call in sick or something too?"

Cullen shrugged. "I haven't heard from him at all, other than a very weird conversation last week. Regarding you, actually." He paused, and when I pulled my gaze away from my laptop, I found Cullen looking at me expectantly. "Did something happen between you two?"

The image of Smith moving on top of me flashed through my brain, and the memory of his naughty game of keep-away where he wouldn't let me touch him burned inside me. The inner thoughts and dreams and fears we'd shared . . . it all felt like a mountain of deceit inside me.

With tears filling my eyes, I grabbed my purse and rose to my feet. "I'm not telling you anything. You're my brother."

Then I stormed from the office, set on hiding out the rest of this decade, safe in my own apartment.

Chapter Twenty-Five

Smith

Four missed calls. Three from Cullen and one from Evie.

Blowing out a sigh, I set my phone down on the table and stared out the window at a young woman pushing a baby stroller down the street.

After what I thought was a great night with Evie, I'd woken up alone yesterday, and I still wasn't sure what to think. Yeah, there had been a sweet note saying she'd had a great time and would see me at work on Monday, but that didn't take away the sting completely. I'd spent my Sunday contemplating whether to call her and find out where her head was at, but had eventually opted to leave it for a day.

It was probably partly my fault that she'd left. I'd meant to tell her how I was feeling, and when we fell asleep in each other's arms, I was sure I'd have time in the morning. Until she'd up and left before I woke.

It had left me in a dark, miserable mood all day. One

that I almost let take over. What if she was like my mother, and the second I decided I was all in, she packed up and walked out? What if what I was feeling was one-sided, and she'd only been in it for the sex, to check that item off her bucket list?

Now, though, as I thought back on it all—the light in her eyes as I moved over her, the warmth in her face when she looked at me—I was confident she'd felt it too. The bond tightening between us that felt more real than anything I'd felt before. The only question was whether she was going to be strong enough to withstand Cullen's disapproval and admit what I already knew, deep down in my bones.

We were meant to be together.

But the thought of going to the office and trying to talk this through with Cullen there made my gut churn.

So I didn't. Instead, I'd slapped my alarm clock off the nightstand and closed my eyes again, determined to get at least another hour of the sleep the Reed family had robbed me of the night before.

I'd managed a whole half hour of sleep before I

climbed out of bed to make a massive decadent breakfast for myself. Pancakes, bacon, the whole nine yards. Then I'd proceeded to eat exactly none of it because Cullen's texts started coming in.

CULLEN: *Where the fuck are you?*

CULLEN: *Pick up the phone, asshole.*

And my personal favorite?

CULLEN: *Real fucking mature.*

Maybe he was right. Not showing up for work hadn't been my finest move, but he was the pot calling the kettle black. How mature was it to try to keep your little sister from having a relationship if she wanted one?

A relationship that just might make her happy if either of them would let it.

I took a swallow of coffee and grimaced. It was cup

number four, and already my empty stomach was feeling bitter with acid. Clearly, something had happened at work if Cullen was so desperate to get in touch, but damn if I knew what. What I did know was that, as much as I liked putting off the inevitable drama, I couldn't just sit here stewing all day either.

Time to face the music, once and for all.

I rushed through a quick shower and dressed for the office, taking a second to scrape my congealed breakfast off the plate and into the garbage before leaving.

On the ride over, I was a mental wreck, wondering if I was going to walk in only to get shit-canned, or if Cullen was going to be waiting on the other side of the office door with boxing gloves on. Neither scenario was out of the question, and I was almost hoping for the latter. It wouldn't be the first time we'd solved a problem with our fists. Hell, it might actually clear the air.

But once I got there and saw Evie's car wasn't in the lot, something in my mind snapped and my whole mentality changed.

I was sick to death of tiptoeing around. This was all

so fucking stupid. There were people in the world with real problems, stuck in abusive relationships or taking care of a loved one with a serious illness. This wedge keeping Evie and me apart was all our own doing. The three of us had put each other into little boxes our whole lives. Evie was my best friend's little sister, but it was only sheer stubbornness on Cullen's part that dictated she couldn't also be my woman.

Enough pussyfooting. I was going to get through to him today and make it official with Evie, or I was going to die trying.

I shoved my way through the doors, each step spring-loaded.

"First things first," I muttered under my breath.

I pushed through the office doors and found Cullen staring down at his phone in irritation. Evie was nowhere to be seen.

Cullen's gaze shot up to meet mine, and he grimaced. "About fucking time you showed up. Thanks for gracing us with your presence."

I flipped him off and turned my desk chair around,

sliding it in front of his desk to straddle it.

"I'm in love with your sister," I said, zero apology in my voice.

Anger rolled off him in palpable waves now, but I was past caring.

"One night when we were in Paris, she came to my hotel room and tried to seduce me," I continued. "Once I realized what was happening, because of our friendship, I put her off. For the past month, I've continued to put her off because I didn't want to cause a rift. Not between me and you, or you and Evie. But now, shit's getting real. I don't just want to sleep with her. I want to wake up with her, and spend the day with her, and share my life with her."

Cullen's face was still stony, but his eyes narrowed a little as he listened intently.

"She's the only person of the opposite sex besides Pam who gets me. She makes me laugh, and she's so smart and caring." I let out a low laugh. "Here I am telling you, but you already know all this. Point is, it took me this long to realize that she's all that and more. Now, I know I haven't always been a relationship guy, but I swear that if you give us your blessing, I will never hurt her. She's the best thing that ever happened to me, Cullen."

He leaned his palm against the desk and cocked his head. "Have you thought about what happens if it doesn't work out, Smith? Then what?"

"It's a risk I'm willing to take if she is. But honestly, man?" I shook my head slowly. "This is it for me. She's the one. So if she'll have me, I'm going to devote everything I've got to making sure it *does* work out. So I'm asking this one time. Can we have your blessing?"

Silence stretched for so long, my hopes started to fall, but then he spoke.

"And if I say no?"

This wasn't a question I wanted to answer, but I was through lying.

"If I have anything to say about it, we're going to do it anyway. That's how much I care. But I know it would go a long way to making your sister happy if you said yes."

Apparently, despite my reservations, that was the

right response.

Cullen shot me a bitter half smile. "All I ever wanted was for her to be happy. Maybe I didn't show it the right way sometimes, but that's the truth. So, yeah." He pushed himself to stand and then made his way around his desk. "You have my blessing. But if you hurt her? You're *also* going to have my foot so far up your ass, people will think you're a boot, understood?"

Some of the ice in my stomach started to melt, and I scrubbed a hand over my jaw in relief. Now hardly seemed like the time to remind him I'd whipped his ass last time we'd sparred, boxing at the gym, so I managed to hold it in.

"Yup, got it," I said with a nod as I stood.

I could tell he was still pissed that I'd hidden it from him, and who could blame him? But as I walked out the door, he called after me.

"Jesus, Smith. Shut the fucking door behind you. What, were you raised by wolves?"

At that, I knew everything would be okay. It might take a little time, but our friendship would survive this.

Now, all I had to do was convince Evie of that.

• • •

I made my way to her apartment, hoping like hell she was home since I had no idea why she wasn't at work today either. Once I got there, I paused for a second outside. Low sobs were muffled by the oak door, making my pulse pound double-time.

I rapped hard once and then pushed it open without waiting for a reply.

"Evie?" I let myself inside and headed for the living room.

She was facedown on the couch, her face buried in her arms, but she startled and sat up when she heard my voice.

"What's wrong? Why are you crying?"

"Smith? I th-thought you weren't going in today," she murmured, swiping a hand over her tear-streaked cheeks with a sniffle. "I told Cullen I wasn't feeling well."

My heart ached at seeing her so upset, and I

approached the couch and then knelt beside her.

"What's the matter?" I asked, taking one of her icy hands in mine and squeezing. It was shitty, but while part of me felt terrible that she was sad, another part of me feared she was crying because she wanted to break things off with me and didn't know how.

"Everything is messed up now. You were too uncomfortable to come to work, and Cullen is furious with me. I was a wreck this morning, wondering where you were." She shook her head miserably. "I wanted you so much, I ignored the fact that us sleeping together would ruin everything. I couldn't sit in the office for another minute today. I'm sure Cullen is pitching a fit right now."

Hot tears splashed on my wrist, and I yanked her up from the couch and into my arms as I stood.

"Shh, stop. Nothing is ruined. In fact, everything is great. Or it can be, if you let it," I murmured, rubbing her back in slow, comforting circles.

She pulled back to gaze up at me and sucked in a shuddering breath. "How can you say that? I can't stop thinking about you, and I doubt that's going to change. So even if Cullen wasn't mad at us both, working side by side will be next to impossible. At least, for me it will. Plus—"

I let out a frustrated growl and crushed my mouth to hers. Fuck, I was sick of talking. Talking was what had us in this mess in the first place. Had we both kept quiet, we'd have consummated our relationship that very first night and probably realized that neither of us would ever have it so good again.

All that time wasted played through my head, and I was done. She stiffened in surprise but then let out a soft moan and circled my neck with her arms.

I slipped my tongue between her lips and pulled her closer to me, reveling in the feel of her breasts against my chest. It wasn't until her muscles were loose and her body fluid around me like melted chocolate that I pulled back.

"Can I get a word in now?" I asked, tracing her bottom lip with my thumb.

She nodded silently.

"It won't be impossible to work side by side, Evie. It's going to be amazing, because now we can at least go out to lunch, and talk on the way in together, and stop hiding."

Her eyes went wide. "W-what do you mean? Cullen—"

"Cullen knows everything. I went to the office before I came to find you, and I laid it all out for him."

"Laid what out?" she asked breathlessly, her bottom lip trembling now.

"I told him that I loved you," I replied, running a hand through her silky curls. "That I would like his blessing but didn't need it, because we were meant to be together."

"You . . . you love me?" she squeaked. Those green eyes that had finally gone clear filled with tears again, and they gleamed like liquid emeralds. "Are you for real?"

"I love you, Everleigh. I love your face, and that sweet smile." I bent her back to expose the column of her neck, punctuating each declaration with kisses down her throat. "I love your brilliant mind and your artistic soul. I love the way you treat my niece and nephews like family when you've only just met."

"What else?" she demanded, her fingers curling into my hair. "What else do you love, Smith?"

Her voice had gone husky, and my cock leaped to attention. "I love the way you call my name when you come," I murmured, sliding a hand up to cover her breast. "I love the way your body squeezes mine when—"

"Hold that thought!" She gasped, tugging free of me and running a hand through her hair as her eyes burned into mine. "I've got you all alone in my place, and I'm not wasting this opportunity. Let's go!"

She grabbed my hand, all but dragging me toward what I assumed was her bedroom.

"Wait, don't you have something to tell me?" I half teased, pulling her to a halt while my cock stood at complete attention.

I knew it. I'd seen the words written all over her face. But, damn it, I wanted to hear them.

Her lips tipped into a radiant smile that warmed me straight to my feet.

"I love you, Smith Hamilton. Now, come on and

fuck me before my brother catches us playing hooky."

Epilogue

Evie

I peeked out the window to see Smith hoisting the last shovelful of snow off the driveway, and my heart did a little dance. I couldn't wait until he came inside. I had freshly made hot cocoa from scratch, and a movie cued up on Netflix. Not to mention some amazing news.

I rushed into the kitchen and added a few marshmallows to our cups, grinning as I did. These were my favorite mugs. Cullen had given them to us as one of his wedding gifts. They said *Mr.* and *Mrs.* in beautiful calligraphy, and each could hold a cup of coffee big enough to choke a horse.

I took a long sip from my mug and let out a sigh. Smith and I had been married for almost a year now, and it had been the adventure of a lifetime so far. Our wedding day had been pure magic. Pam had graciously allowed the kids to share in the ring-bearer duties as Winnie didn't want to be a flower girl. They'd all worn capes by request, except Mac, who had nearly worn nothing at all as he tried to strip off his miniature tuxedo pants halfway down the aisle.

I grinned at the memory. Cullen had been the best man, and Maggie had been my maid of honor. Whatever tension had arisen between Smith and Cullen over our secret had long since faded away, and Cullen's sweet but funny best-man speech had solidified it. They were back to their old selves like it had never even happened. I couldn't have lived with myself any other way, so I was thrilled about that.

The day after the wedding, we'd gone on a whirlwind trip to Italy, and had toured the countryside together. I'd loved traveling alone and with friends, but with Smith, everything seemed to take on a whole new life. Now, each new place we visited was tied to a memory. We were a family of two, and we were building the life I'd always dreamed of having.

Cullen was still hard at work, taking over the world, and the business was booming. It was especially sweet for me because I knew I was a part of the reason for that success. My advertising campaigns had been integral in building a new client base, and Cullen had hired two people to work under me so I could continue to assist in the expansion.

The front door swung open, cutting into my thoughts, and I carried the mugs into the living room with a smile. Smith stepped inside and stomped his boots on the mat in front of the door.

"It's officially November in Chicago," he said with a laugh. "There's got to be about fifteen inches out there."

He tugged off his gloves and stripped off his coat as I stepped toward him, his mug extended.

"Well, I've got something hot to warm you up," I murmured, rolling up onto my tiptoes to give him a kiss.

He didn't take the mug, though. Instead, he yanked me closer and I let out a squeak.

"I think I know exactly how you can do that," he murmured, crushing his mouth to mine. The mugs were quickly forgotten as he slipped his tongue against mine.

His lips were cold, but I didn't care. Even a year in, it still felt like a dream that I could kiss and touch and make love with this man whenever I wanted to, and I wasn't going to squander it.

I pulled away and set the mugs onto the side table.

"I think I might be able to help you out there, mister. We can heat those mugs up later."

We all but ran into the bedroom and stripped each other with the efficiency of longtime lovers, but our urgency stopped there. My tongue stuck to the roof of my mouth as I stared at his naked body. He still managed to make my knees weak every time.

"You are fine as hell, Mr. Hamilton," I said, shaking my head in awe.

"You too, Mrs. Hamilton," he replied, tracing the neckline of the lingerie I was wearing.

It had only taken a couple months of Smith telling me how much he loved my body for me to really start to believe him. Over the past year, I'd taken to getting samples of most of the new designs from the office to "test them out." Smith had sighed and said it was a tough job, but someone had to do it. It was the look in his eyes that killed me, though. Whenever he realized I was wearing something new, he lit up like a kid at Christmas.

"Red. I like," Smith said, cupping my breasts through

the silk.

The fabric and the pressure of his fingers felt amazing against my skin, and I let my eyes slide shut.

My head fell back as he bent in to close his teeth gently over my neck. Cupping the back of his head, I held him close and whispered his name. He walked me backward in tiny steps until my legs met the mattress, and then he pressed me down onto it. I dragged him with me so his body covered mine, and for a second, I just relished the warm weight of him. But that didn't satisfy me for long. I rolled him off me and climbed over him, lining up my center with his hard cock. A muscle in his jaw flexed as he watched me through hooded eyes.

"That negligee looks dead sexy on you. Let's leave it on," he said, a glint in his eyes as he flicked a thumb over my nipple.

"I think that sounds like a great idea." I was already hiking up the fabric so I could feel his heated flesh against mine. We gasped in unison as his cock touched my slick folds.

"You feel so good," I groaned, sliding back and

forth, wetting him with my juices.

He clutched my hips in his hands and worked me over him faster. The friction between us was making my whole body tremble, and suddenly, I couldn't wait to get him inside me. I rose up on my knees until I was poised over him and took his shaft in hand. Then I slid down, taking all of his massive length at once. The breath left my lungs in a whoosh, and my vision went hazy.

"God, you fill me all the way up. It's so good, Smith," I whispered, rocking slowly at first, and then more quickly as my body adjusted to his size.

He watched in rapt attention as I moved up and down, folding his hands behind his head with a smirk as he enjoyed the show. Emboldened, I slid one strap off my shoulder and then the other, tugging the sweetheart neckline of the negligee down just enough that my breasts popped out the top of it.

"Fuck, yeah," Smith growled as he stared. "Love watching you ride my cock."

His dirty talk never failed to make me wetter, and I moaned as I quickened the pace even more.

"Fuck me, Evie. Take that cock deep and ride it until you come for me, baby," he urged, his fingers tightening on my hips in a punishing grip.

The erotic drag of his rock-hard cock in and out, faster and faster, had me tossing my head back and crying out his name.

Close. So close.

And then his fingers were between us and he was massaging my clit.

"That's it, baby. Take what you need."

He groaned as my hips pounded up and down, driving him so deep inside me that stars exploded behind my eyelids. And then I was flying, calling out his name in a hoarse cry as a climax rocketed through me. It shook me to the core, and wave after wave of ecstasy crashed over me. I was still coming when Smith's muscles tensed beneath me.

"Yes," I moaned, encouraging him breathlessly. "Come inside me."

He gritted his teeth and his back arched, wedging his

cock as far as it would go as he exploded, spurting inside me in a hot rush.

For a long moment we stayed like that, riding out the aftershocks together, caressing each other softly until we finally came down.

"Well, you definitely warmed me up," he murmured, still breathing hard as he tugged me to his side. "If this is the treatment I get for shoveling, I'm going to have to do some sort of snow dance so we get more."

I smiled and shook my head. "Please don't. We've got two more weeks before we leave for Hawaii, and I don't want our flights getting canceled."

"True," he agreed. "We definitely need some sunshine in our lives. I can already taste the pineapple piña coladas."

"Yeah, we have to make the most of it. We won't be traveling for a while after that, though," I murmured, lazily toying with the trail of hair below his belly button.

He pulled back to shoot a puzzled glance down at me. "What do you mean? I thought you wanted to try to get to Paris in the summer."

"I do. But it will probably be tough traveling with an infant, you know? I'm thinking we should wait until next spring."

He stared at me, nonplussed, for a full thirty seconds. Then his cheeks went pale.

For a moment, my heart skipped and I was terrified. It never occurred to me that he wouldn't be as ecstatic as I was about the news. But then he let out a whoop.

"Are you serious, Evie? Are you dead fucking serious right now?"

I nodded, and happy tears flooded my eyes. "I am. I bought the test last night and did it this morning when you were out shoveling. I even bought a spare to double-check. It's positive. We're having a baby, Smith."

He pulled me over on top of him and held me fast against his body as he stroked my hair. "I love Pam's kids, and I knew I'd be excited to have my own one day, but I never thought it could feel like this. I'm humbled and just . . ."

The emotion in his voice had made it husky, and the awe in it made me cry harder.

"You've made me so happy," he said softly. "I finally feel like my life is complete. Like I'm a part of something bigger than myself." He kissed my shoulder and then released his hold on me. "Shit! Am I squeezing too tight? I don't want to squish my kid."

I chuckled and yanked his arms back around me. "No way, José. You better keep squeezing me. I'm sure the baby loves it."

"Sometimes I lie awake at night and watch you sleep, and I wonder what would've happened if you hadn't come into my hotel room that night." He stroked my cheek gently. "And it makes my insides go cold. What if I was too stupid to come to you, Evie? We might never have found this."

"Well, I guess it's a good thing one of us is a risk taker then, isn't it?" I teased.

He let out a bark of laughter and started tickling me.

It was official. Daredevil Evie Knievel had successfully pulled off one of the most spectacular death-defying stunts ever.

The prize?

A lifetime of happiness.

Also Available in The Roommates Series

THE HOUSE MATE

What's sexier than a bad boy? A badass man who's got his shit together.

Max Alexander is nearing thirty-five. He's built a successful company and has conquered the professional world, but he's never been lucky in love. Since he's focused so much time on his business and raising his daughter, adulting has come at the expense of his personal life.

His social skills are shit, his patience is shot, and at times, his temper runs hot.

The last thing he has time for is the recently single, too-gorgeous-for-her-own-good young woman he hires to take care of his little girl. She's a distraction he doesn't need, and besides, there's no way she'd be interested. But you know what they say about assumptions?

THE ROOM MATE

The last time I saw my best friend's younger brother, he was a geek wearing braces. But when Cannon shows up to crash in my spare room, I get a swift reality check.

Now twenty-four, he's broad shouldered and masculine, and so sinfully sexy, I want to climb him like the jungle gyms we used to enjoy. At six-foot-something with lean muscles hiding under his T-shirt, a deep sexy voice, and full lips that pull into a smirk when he studies me, he's pure temptation.

Fresh out of a messy breakup, he doesn't want any entanglements. But I can resist, right?

I'm holding strong until the third night of our new arrangement when we get drunk and he confesses his biggest secret of all: he's cursed when it comes to sex. Apparently he's a god in bed, and women instantly fall in love with him.

I'm calling bullshit. In fact, I'm going to prove him wrong, and if I rack up a few much-needed orgasms in the process, all the better.

There's no way I'm going to fall in love with Cannon. But once we start…I realize betting against him may have been the biggest mistake of my life.

Acknowledgments

I'm so grateful to my wonderful team members, who each played a role in helping to whip this book into shape.

Thank you to Danielle Sanchez, publicist extraordinaire, who deserves a trophy for putting up with me on a daily basis.

Thank you to the amazing Pam Berehulke, whose editing talents make my writing shine, and to my critique partner, Rachel Brookes, for being an amazing sounding board and cheerleader.

Thank you to Alyssa Garcia, who has already proven to be a lifesaver in such a short time.

And of course, thank you to the best readers in the whole wide world, romance readers! To those of you who seek happily-ever-afters, both in real life and on the page, I stand here proudly with you.

Stay Connected

Sign up for my private mailing list to be updated when I have a new release or a sale.

www.kendallryanbooks.com/newsletter.

About the Author

A New York Times, Wall Street Journal, and USA Today bestselling author of more than two dozen titles, Kendall Ryan has sold over 2 million books and her books have been translated into several languages in countries around the world. Her books have also appeared on the New York Times and USA Today bestseller lists more than three dozen times. Ryan has been featured in such publications as USA Today, Newsweek, and InTouch Magazine. She lives in Texas with her husband and two sons.

Website

www.kendallryanbooks.com

Other Books by Kendall Ryan

Unravel Me

Make Me Yours

Hard to Love

The Impact of You

Resisting Her

Working It

Craving Him

All or Nothing

The When I Break Series

The Filthy Beautiful Lies Series

The Gentleman Mentor

Sinfully Mine

Screwed

Bait & Switch

Slow & Steady

Wednesday

Hitched, Volumes 1-3

The Fix Up

The Room Mate

The House Mate

The Soul Mate